AIDS AND HEALTH ISSUES

≋ AFRICA: PROGRESS & PROBLEMS ≋

AIDS AND HEALTH ISSUES

LeeAnne Gelletly

Mason Crest Publishers
Philadelphia

Frontispiece: A Ugandan Ministry of Health inspector reviews records with a hospital doctor, Kampala.

Produced by OTTN Publishing, Stockton, New Jersey

Mason Crest Publishers
370 Reed Road
Broomall, PA 19008
www.masoncrest.com

3 5 7 9 8 6 4 2

Library of Congress Cataloging-in-Publication Data

Gelletly, LeeAnne.
  AIDS and health issues in Africa / LeeAnne Gelletly.
    p. cm. — (Africa, progress and problems)
  Includes bibliographical references and index.
  ISBN-13: 978-1-59084-954-5
  ISBN-10: 1-59084-954-X
  1. AIDS (Disease)—Africa. I. Title. II. Series.
  RA643.86.A35G45 2006
  362.196'9792'0096—dc22
                    2005023101

TABLE OF CONTENTS

AFRICA: PROGRESS & PROBLEMS

AIDS AND HEALTH ISSUES

CIVIL WARS IN AFRICA

ECOLOGICAL ISSUES

EDUCATION IN AFRICA

ETHNIC GROUPS IN AFRICA

GOVERNANCE AND LEADERSHIP
IN AFRICA

HELPING AFRICA HELP ITSELF:
A GLOBAL EFFORT

HUMAN RIGHTS IN AFRICA

ISLAM IN AFRICA

THE MAKING OF MODERN AFRICA

POPULATION AND OVERCROWDING

POVERTY AND ECONOMIC ISSUES

RELIGIONS OF AFRICA

THE PROMISE OF TODAY'S AFRICA

by Robert I. Rotberg

Today's Africa is a mosaic of effective democracy and desperate despotism, immense wealth and abysmal poverty, conscious modernity and mired traditionalism, bitter conflict and vast arenas of peace, and enormous promise and abiding failure. Generalizations are more difficult to apply to Africa or Africans than elsewhere. The continent, especially the sub-Saharan two-thirds of its immense landmass, presents enormous physical, political, and human variety. From snow-capped peaks to intricate patches of remaining jungle, from desolate deserts to the greatest rivers, and from the highest coastal sand dunes anywhere to teeming urban conglomerations, Africa must be appreciated from myriad perspectives. Likewise, its peoples come in every shape and size, govern themselves in several complicated manners, worship a host of indigenous and imported gods, and speak thousands of original and five or six derivative common languages. To know Africa is to know nuance and complexity.

There are 53 nation-states that belong to the African Union, 48 of which are situated within the sub-Saharan mainland or on its offshore islands. No other continent has so many countries, political divisions, or members of the General Assembly of the United Nations. No other continent encompasses so many distinctively different peoples or spans such geographical disparity. On no other continent have so many innocent civilians lost their lives in intractable civil wars—12 million since 1991 in such places as Algeria, Angola, the Congo, Côte d'Ivoire, Liberia, Sierra Leone, and the Sudan. No other continent has so many disparate natural resources (from cadmium, cobalt, and copper to petroleum and zinc) and so little to show for their frenzied exploitation. No other continent has proportionally so many people subsisting (or trying to) on less than $1 a day. But then no other continent has been so beset by HIV/AIDS (30 percent of all adults in southern Africa), by tuberculosis, by malaria (prevalent almost everywhere), and by less well-known scourges such as schistosomiasis (liver fluke), several kinds of filariasis, river blindness, trachoma, and trypanosomiasis (sleeping sickness).

Africa is the most Christian continent. It has more Muslims than the Middle East. Apostolic and Pentecostal churches are immensely powerful. So are Sufi brotherhoods. Yet traditional African religions are still influential. So is a belief in spirits and witches (even among Christians and Muslims), in faith healing and in alternative medicine. Polygamy remains popular. So does the practice of female circumcision and other long-standing cultural preferences. Africa cannot be well understood without appreciating how village life still permeates the great cities and how urban pursuits engulf villages. Half if not more of its peoples live in towns and cities; no longer can Africa be considered predominantly rural, agricultural, or wild.

Political leaders must cater to both worlds, old and new. They and their followers must join the globalized, Internet-penetrated world even as they remain rooted appropriately in past modes of behavior, obedient to dictates of family, lineage, tribe, and ethnicity. This duality often results in democracy or at least partially participatory democracy. Equally often it develops into autocracy. Botswana and Mauritius have enduring democratic governments. In Benin, Ghana, Kenya, Lesotho, Malawi, Mali, Mozambique, Namibia, Nigeria, Senegal, South Africa, Tanzania, and Zambia fully democratic pursuits are relatively recent and not yet sustainably implanted. Algeria, Cameroon, Chad, the Central African Republic, Egypt, the Sudan, and Tunisia are authoritarian entities run by strongmen. Zimbabweans and Equatorial Guineans suffer from even more venal rule. Swazis and Moroccans are subject to the real whims of monarchs. Within even this vast sweep of political practice there are still more distinctions. The partial democracies represent a spectrum. So does the manner in which authority is wielded by kings, by generals, and by long-entrenched civilian autocrats.

The democratic countries are by and large better developed and more rapidly growing economically than those ruled by strongmen. In Africa there is an association between the pursuit of good governance and beneficial economic performance. Likewise, the natural resource wealth curse that has afflicted mineral-rich countries such as the Congo and Nigeria has had the opposite effect in well-governed places like Botswana. Nation-states open to global trade have done better than those with closed economies. So have those countries with prudent managements, sensible fiscal arrangements, and modest deficits. Overall, however, the bulk of African countries have suffered in terms of reduced economic growth from the sheer fact of being tropical, beset by disease in an enervating climate where there is an average of one trained physician to every 13,000 persons. Many lose growth prospects, too, because of the absence of navigable rivers, the paucity of ocean and river ports, barely maintained roads, and few and narrow railroads. Moreover, 15 of Africa's countries are landlocked, without comfortable access to relatively inexpensive waterborne transport. Hence, imports and exports for much of Africa are more expensive than elsewhere as they move over formidable distances. Africa is the most underdeveloped continent because of geographical and health constraints that have not yet been overcome, because of ill-considered policies, because of the sheer number of separate nation-states (a colonial legacy), and because of poor governance.

Africa's promise is immense, and far more exciting than its achievements have been since a wave of nationalism and independence in the 1960s liberated nearly every section of the continent. Thus, the next several decades of the 21st century are ones of promise for Africa. The challenges are clear: to alleviate grinding poverty and deliver greater real economic goods to larger proportions of people in each country, and across all 53 countries; to deliver more of the benefits of good governance to more of Africa's peoples; to end the destructive killing fields that run rampant across so much of Africa; to improve educational training and health services; and to roll back the scourges of HIV/AIDS, tuberculosis, and malaria. Every challenge represents an opportunity with concerted and bountiful Western assistance to transform the lives of Africa's vulnerable and resourceful future generations.

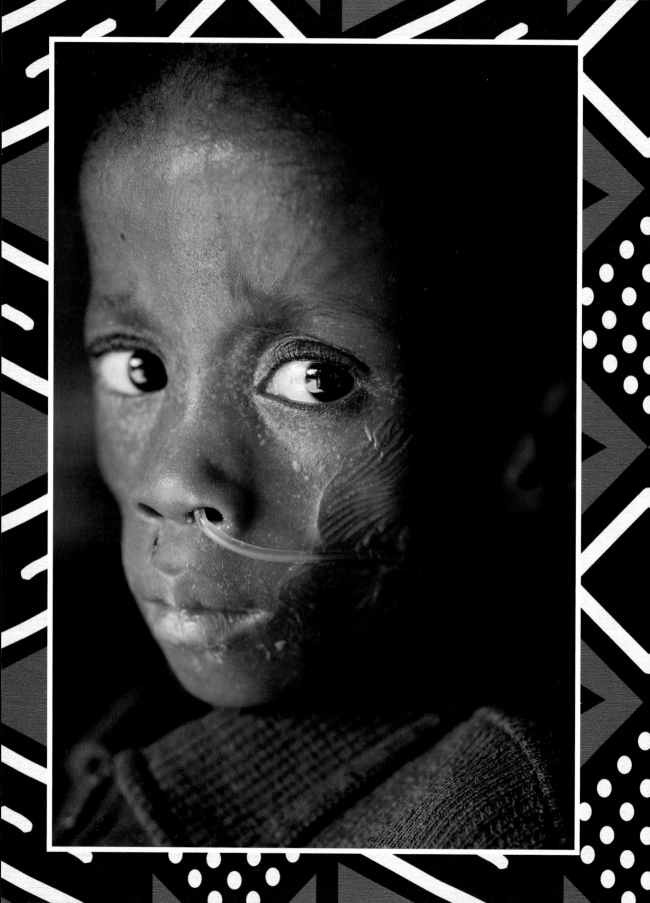

1 OVERVIEW: AFRICA'S HEALTH CRISIS

Of the approximately 6.5 billion people living in the world today, almost half will die before age 45 because of infectious diseases. Many of these deaths occur in Africa, where infectious diseases remain the number-one killer.

LIVES CUT SHORT

During the 1960s and 1970s, many African countries had effective public health systems. During those decades the average African could expect to live until the age of 62.

However, since the 1980s, the average lifespan of Africa's citizens has fallen dramatically. As of 2000 life expectancy in sub-Saharan Africa (the region south of the Sahara Desert) had plummeted to 47 years—22 years less than the average lifespan of people living in East Asia (69 years) and 31 years lower than the average age at death in industrial nations (78 years). Although famine, accidents, and warfare and civil unrest account for some of Africa's premature deaths,

The face of affliction: This eight-year-old in Cape Town, South Africa, is HIV-positive and has tuberculosis, an opportunistic disease often associated with AIDS. The HIV/AIDS pandemic has visited untold misery on sub-Saharan Africa.

much of this decrease in life expectancy is due to infectious diseases.

The greatest killer has been AIDS (acquired immune deficiency syndrome), an incurable disease caused by the human immunodeficiency virus, or HIV. This virus weakens the body's immune system so that it cannot fight off infections. While AIDS has spread across the globe since the first cases were identified in the early 1980s, the people of Africa—particularly sub-Saharan Africa—have clearly suffered the most. Of the more than 25 million lives lost worldwide to the AIDS pandemic by 2005, approximately 17 million were Africans, the majority from countries south of the Sahara Desert. Sub-Saharan Africans also accounted for some 25.8 million of the estimated 40.3 million people living with HIV, according to the *AIDS Epidemic Update* published in December 2005 by the World Health Organization (WHO) and the Joint United Nations Program on HIV/AIDS (UNAIDS). Although Sub-Saharan Africa contains only about 10 percent of the world's population, it accounts for more than 60 percent of all HIV/AIDS cases.

HIV/AIDS has devastated southern African countries, where up to one-third of the adult population (defined as persons aged 15 to 49) lives with the disease. Botswana suffers the highest adult prevalence rate: an estimated 38.8 percent of its citizens in the 15–49 age group are infected with HIV. In 2004 the UN reported that life expectancy in nine southern African countries (Botswana, Central African Republic, Lesotho, Malawi, Mozambique, Rwanda, Swaziland, Zambia, and Zimbabwe) had fallen below 40 years.

The second-deadliest disease in sub-Saharan Africa is malaria. This vector-borne illness has been controlled or eliminated in many other parts of the world, but not in sub-Saharan Africa. Almost 90 percent of the world's malaria deaths occur in this region. The number-one killer of African children, malaria causes the deaths of up to a million children—and possibly as many as 3 million—each year.

Africa's third greatest killer disease, tuberculosis (TB), has reemerged on the continent because of HIV/AIDS. Weakened immune systems have been unable to fend off growing tuberculosis bacterial infections. The number of tuberculosis cases in Africa has increased fivefold since AIDS was first identified in the early 1980s. The rapid course of TB has been relentless: the number of annual deaths from the disease in Africa exploded from 200,000 in 1990 to 540,000 in 2005. Today, tuberculosis in Africa accounts for 25 percent of the world's cases, and that percentage is increasing.

POVERTY AND DISEASE

In large part, Africans have been vulnerable to these three deadly diseases because they are extremely poor. Most African countries are developing nations, or countries in which the majority of people live in poverty. According to the United Nations Conference on Trade and Development, almost 9 out of 10 people in the continent's poorest countries live on an income of less than $2 per day. About two-thirds live in extreme poverty, defined as an income of $1 per day or less per person. In such households, families cannot meet their basic needs for survival (food, health care, safe drinking water and sanitation, shelter, clothing), and the lack of these necessities has compromised their health.

The sub-Saharan region of Africa contains the most people living in extreme poverty. With insufficient food and chronic hunger, many suffer from malnutrition, which stunts the growth and development of children, and leaves both adults and children weak and susceptible to the infectious illnesses that often rage around them. An estimated one of every three children in Africa is underweight, and more than a fourth of Africa's people are chronically malnourished.

Extreme poverty also means that when people fall ill, they often don't get treatment. Many impoverished and isolated rural areas lack health care professionals and facilities to diagnose and treat serious diseases. And even where a functioning medical system is in place, many African households cannot afford treatment. Drugs to slow the progression of HIV/AIDS, for example, are prohibitively expensive, as are treatments that can cure malaria and tuberculosis. According to the 2005 *AIDS Epidemic Update*, only 1 in 10 HIV-infected people living in Africa could obtain lifesaving treatments.

Disease and poverty can be a vicious circle, explains Jeffrey Sachs in his book *The End of Poverty: Economic Possibilities for Our Time:* "Poor health causes poverty and poverty contributes to poor health." If the sick seek care from a health center or clinic, they become even poorer because they must pay for treatment by borrowing money or selling off their belongings—often the tools and livestock necessary for their livelihood. The severe illness of a family wage earner who can no longer work also results in lost household income.

Poverty also facilitates the transmission of disease through population displacement. When people cannot support their families in impoverished rural areas, they gravitate toward cities in search of jobs. Crowded and often unsanitary living conditions typically await these economic migrants in the cities, and infectious diseases spread readily under such conditions. When

Mothers and children waiting for food at a relief center in Ethiopia. Africa's health crisis is inextricably linked with issues of poverty.

workers return to their villages to visit their families, they often carry infections back with them.

LACK OF SAFE DRINKING WATER

Disease also spreads easily through Africa because much of the water that people drink is contaminated with bacteria, viruses, parasites, or other pathogens. Among the most life-threatening waterborne diseases are cholera, schistosomiasis, and typhoid fever.

Such diseases remain common in Africa because more than half of the continent's population lacks access to safe drinking water and adequate sanitation services. In some rural areas, people have to walk several hours to reach the closest source of water, which often is dangerously polluted by animal waste or agricultural runoff. Large numbers of Africans forced from their homes by civil war, drought, or famine are also

More than half of Africa's people lack access to clean water and are therefore at risk of contracting diseases caused by waterborne parasites and pathogens. The situation is especially serious in the continent's overcrowded refugee and displaced-person camps. This photo shows a displaced-person camp in Liberia.

vulnerable to waterborne diseases. Many overcrowded refugee and displaced-person camps have insufficient supplies of clean water (and often food), along with inadequate sanitation and poor medical care—creating conditions that are ideal for the spread of waterborne diseases and other contagious infections such as yellow fever and meningitis.

The rapid growth of Africa's major cities has also contributed to the spread of infectious diseases. In 1950 only one-seventh of the African population lived in cities; as of 2000, two-fifths were living in urban areas. Today, there are more than 30 African cities with populations of over 1 million, and many of their inhabitants live in shantytowns and slums. Explosive growth has overwhelmed existing sewage and water systems, creating severely polluted waters that are hotbeds for infectious diseases.

BUDGETARY CONSTRAINTS

The economies of many low-income African nations have declined significantly since the 1980s, depriving governments of financial resources that could be used to provide much-needed health care services or to fund education programs to slow the spread of diseases such as HIV/AIDS. Limited public health budgets have also taken a toll on the basic infrastructure to control disease: training of medical workers and volunteers, immunization programs, and medical facilities. In some cases, the lack of public health funds has forced governments that previously offered free health care to charge for such services. As a result, the extremely poor have lost access to health care entirely.

Debt has contributed significantly to the inability of African governments to meet the health care needs of their people. During the 1990s and the early years of the 21st century, as Africa's developing countries struggled to cope with devastating disease epidemics such as HIV/AIDS, they also had to make payments on multibillion-dollar loans from Western countries and international financial institutions such as the World Bank, International Monetary Fund (IMF), and African Development Bank. For countries with already weakened economies, servicing their massive debts presented a crushing financial burden, and many governments were forced to divert funds from domestic priorities such as public health budgets. The public health systems in some African countries were also weakened by mismanagement and malfeasance on the part of incompetent and corrupt national leaders.

By 2005 Africa's total debt stood at some $295 billion. Advocates had long argued for debt relief, contending that this

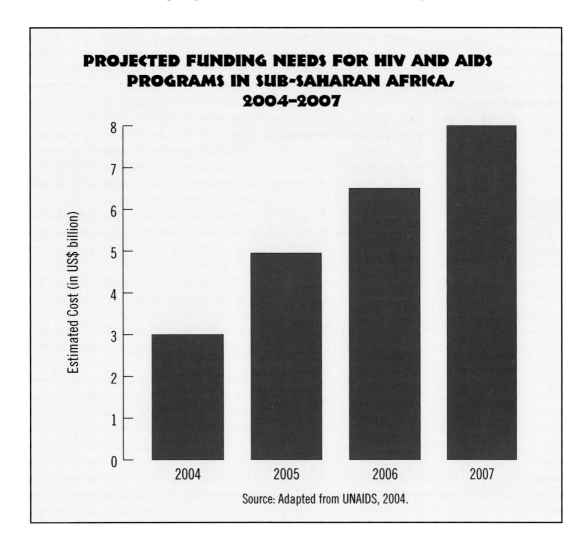

PROJECTED FUNDING NEEDS FOR HIV AND AIDS PROGRAMS IN SUB-SAHARAN AFRICA, 2004–2007

Source: Adapted from UNAIDS, 2004.

would free up funds for impoverished nations to spend on development and social programs such as public health and disease prevention initiatives. In July 2005 the Group of Eight—which comprises the world's major industrialized nations—decided to endorse debt relief. After a meeting in Scotland, leaders of the G8 countries (the United States, Great Britain, Germany, Japan, Italy, France, Russia, and Canada) agreed to write off billions of dollars in loans that the World Bank, IMF, and African Development Bank had made to developing countries. The following September the World Bank and IMF signed on to the plan, which would cancel up to $57.5 billion in debt, most of it owed by nations in Africa, including Benin, Burkina Faso, Ethiopia, Ghana, Madagascar, Mali, Mauritania, Mozambique, Niger, Rwanda, Senegal, Tanzania, Uganda, and Zambia.

HUMANITARIAN EFFORTS

For several decades, African countries have received humanitarian support from organizations and agencies outside the continent. The United Nations works through its various agencies to address pressing issues in Africa, particularly the continent's high rates of hunger and disease. Among the many UN agencies directly involved in such programs are the United Nations Children's Fund (UNICEF), which promotes children's health; the World Health Organization, which works in public health and disease control; and the World Food Program (WFP), which helps feed the world's refugees and displaced people.

These specialized agencies are also represented in UNAIDS. This agency works to address the world AIDS pandemic.

Many other organizations and groups from around the world, including churches, charity organizations, nongovernmental organizations (NGOs), and medical aid groups, have dedicated staff and volunteers working to help Africa battle disease and malnutrition. Some, such as Médicins Sans Frontières (MSF; also called Doctors Without Borders), Oxfam, the Red Cross, and Save the Children, train local and volunteer doctors, nurses, and assistants to diagnose and treat patients; help deliver medications and medical equipment; and establish nutritional programs.

Former U.S. presidents have also founded organizations to aid Africa in the fight against disease. In 1982 Jimmy Carter founded the Carter Center, a nonprofit public policy institute that focuses on human rights and global health needs. The Carter Center has spurred efforts that have dramatically reduced Guinea worm disease in Africa, and it has led campaigns to fight

A nurse uses a video to teach a young mother about health issues at a clinic in South Africa funded by the United States Agency for International Development (USAID).

river blindness, trachoma, lymphatic filariasis, and schistosomiasis. Bill Clinton heads the Clinton Foundation, established in 2002. Its efforts focus on helping governments in Africa, the Caribbean, and Asia provide care, treatment, and prevention programs for HIV/AIDS.

The Centers for Disease Control and Prevention (CDC), a U.S. government agency, is also involved in infectious-disease monitoring and prevention in Africa. Similar work is performed by the UN's World Health Organization.

Despite the efforts of many agencies and organizations to combat disease in Africa, large numbers of Africans are still suffering.

A TRAGIC TOLL

The toll that AIDS, malaria, tuberculosis, and other infectious diseases have taken on Africa is enormous. A great proportion of the victims are children. Sub-Saharan Africa suffers the highest child mortality rate in the world: one out of every five children there dies before reaching age five. And for every 1,000 infants born alive, 118 do not live to see their first birthday. In many cases, these children die from health problems that can be treated, including malnutrition, diarrheal diseases, and vaccine-preventable diseases such as measles and tetanus. The loss of these children means the loss of future workers, farmers, teachers, and community and government leaders for Africa.

The premature deaths of millions of adult workers from disease, particularly AIDS, threatens the economies of many African nations. According to the United Nations Food and Agriculture Organization, AIDS has killed 7 million agricultural workers in 25 African countries since 1985, contributing to severe food shortages. With the loss of farmers, fewer crops are being grown to provide for Africa's people. And with the loss of teachers and medical professionals, fewer children can benefit from an education and fewer sick people can be treated.

The AIDS pandemic has orphaned approximately 11 million children in sub-Saharan Africa. Some are taken in by uncles, aunts, and grandparents—but often these adults also fall ill and die. Those with no adult to care for them must support themselves. Some drop out of school and join the growing ranks of street children, often roving in gangs engaged in petty crime. Still others turn to the sex trade to get money for food and shelter—behavior that leaves them at risk for contracting HIV themselves.

The economic uncertainty and social disruption resulting from the AIDS pandemic and from many other lethal diseases prevalent in Africa threaten the continent's very future. Until these health issues can be effectively addressed, they will continue to erode Africa's economic and social foundations.

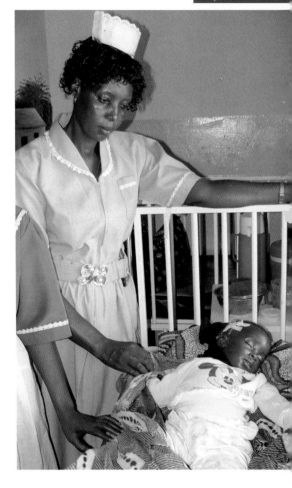

A nurse tends to a sick child at a hospital in Sierra Leone. One of every five children in sub-Saharan Africa dies before reaching his or her fifth birthday.

THE HIV/AIDS PANDEMIC

The human immunodeficiency virus (HIV), which causes AIDS, is the leading infectious disease threat in the world today. While more than 25 million people have died from AIDS since the early 1980s, that number is expected to reach 45 million by 2010. The fourth-biggest killer in the world, HIV/AIDS is the leading cause of death in sub-Saharan Africa.

HIV/AIDS

Scientists believe that HIV evolved from viruses that first infected monkeys and apes in Africa, and that people contracted the disease when they ate these animals as "bushmeat." Once the virus infected people, it was transmitted from human to human through bodily fluids—as a sexually transmitted disease, through contaminated needles or blood, or from mother to child at birth. In Africa, HIV has been transmitted mostly among heterosexual men and women.

(Opposite) HIV/AIDS, the leading cause of death in sub-Saharan Africa, is especially rampant in the southern part of the continent. In South Africa, the home of this patient, about 20 percent of the people in the 15–49 age group are believed to be HIV-positive.

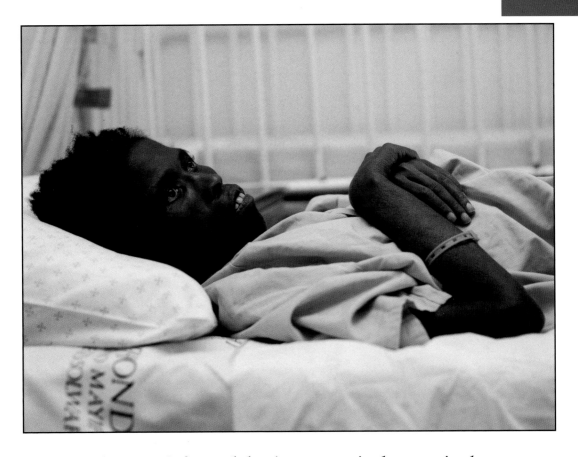

When the virus infects adults, it can remain dormant in the body for 7 to 11 years. During this time, however, the HIV-infected person can transmit the disease to others.

There are two main types of HIV: HIV-1 and HIV-2. The HIV-1 strain has several important subtypes, referred to as A, B, C, and E. The main killer, and the subtype that is predominant in Africa, is HIV-1C. West Africa accounts for high levels of HIV-2 as well.

SYMPTOMS AND TREATMENT

HIV is a lentivirus that infects and destroys the immune system's T cells. Their loss weakens the ability of the body to fight infection, which makes a person vulnerable to attack from diseases that normally do not occur in people with healthy immune systems. Some of the opportunistic infections associated with

AIDS include lung diseases, cancers, tuberculosis, fungal infections, diarrhea, rashes, and lesions.

Opportunistic infections often cause immense suffering for the AIDS victim, and they may last for weeks, and even months, before causing death. Such infections often produce symptoms such as fever, nausea, breathlessness from fluid-filled lungs, and numerous sores that line the throat or cover the body. AIDS depletes the body's protein, causing muscles to waste away; numbs nerve endings in the body's extremities; and attacks the central nervous system, causing it to deteriorate in some cases to the point of dementia.

Although there is no cure for HIV/AIDS and no vaccine to prevent infection, the virus can be treated. Antiretroviral (ARV) drugs have been shown to slow the progression of HIV, make it less contagious, and allow the patient to lead a long, fairly normal life. Once a person with AIDS starts antiretroviral treatment, it must continue for life. If the patient discontinues therapy or takes the medications on an irregular schedule, they lose their effectiveness because drug-resistant strains of the virus evolve.

By the late 1990s, antiretrovirals were the usual method of treatment for AIDS patients in industrialized countries, and their use greatly improved the survival rate of HIV-positive individuals. Antiretroviral therapy also helped HIV-positive patients ward off opportunistic infections. However, antiretroviral treatments are expensive—costing, on average, more than $2,700 per patient annually, according to the World Bank. The drugs are not readily available in developing countries.

PREVENTING AIDS

Because HIV is transmitted in bodily fluids, methods for preventing infection involve avoiding sexual contact with infected individuals or using condoms during sexual activity. Studies have shown that condom use can prevent transmission of HIV.

To prevent transmission of the virus by blood, drug users should not share hypodermic needles. Health care workers in hospitals and clinics need to follow sterile procedures, since a contaminated blood supply and improperly sterilized needles and surgical equipment can spread the disease among patients. HIV is rendered harmless by bleach, alcohol, or soap and water, and it does not survive for more than a few hours upon contact with air.

African children most commonly develop AIDS after transmission of HIV from their infected mothers during pregnancy, during delivery, or from breast feeding. However, if an HIV-positive pregnant woman is given the antiretroviral drug zidovudine, also known as AZT, the odds that she will pass the virus on to her child are reduced. Doctors have also found that the antiretroviral drug nevirapine reduces the possibility of mother-to-child transmission. It must be administered to the woman just before she gives birth and to the infant within the first 48 hours of life. Without antiretroviral medicines, about 35 percent of children born to HIV-positive women contract the virus.

RAPID SPREAD

Since first being identified in the early 1980s, AIDS has swept through sub-Saharan Africa. In 1982 Uganda had the highest adult prevalence rate for HIV. That year, an estimated 2 percent of Ugandans

A peer educator in Senegal stresses the importance of condom use in preventing the spread of HIV.

aged 15 to 49 were HIV-positive. Just 18 years later, 21 African countries were thought to have adult prevalence rates of higher than 7 percent. And as of 2005, HIV adult prevalence for sub-Saharan Africa as a whole stood at an estimated 7.2 percent.

It must be emphasized, however, that HIV prevalence varies widely across sub-Saharan Africa, with southern African nations suffering especially high rates of infection. According to the *2004 Report on the Global AIDS Epidemic*, produced by UNAIDS, at least six southern African countries—Botswana, Lesotho, Namibia, South Africa, Swaziland, and Zimbabwe—had estimated HIV adult prevalence rates higher than 20 percent as of year's end 2003. In Swaziland and Botswana, the estimated proportion of HIV-infected adults approached 4 in 10 (38.8 percent and 37.3 percent, respectively).

In contrast, estimated HIV adult prevalence in the countries of East Africa ranged from 4.1 percent in Uganda to 8.8 percent in Tanzania, according to the UNAIDS report. In Kenya, where up to 15 percent of adults had previously been thought to be HIV-positive, a large-scale government survey conducted in 2003 put the rate at 6.7 percent.

In the countries of West Africa and Central Africa, HIV adult prevalence rates generally range up to about 5 percent. Rates are higher in Côte d'Ivoire (7 percent) and Cameroon (6.9 percent), according to the *2004 Report on the Global AIDS Epidemic*.

HIV/AIDS has not devastated the Arab countries of northern Africa, where the disease prevalence is quite low. In Morocco, Western Sahara, Mauritania, Algeria, Tunisia, Libya, and Egypt, only about 0.1 percent of individuals aged 15 to 49 are infected. Sudan's HIV adult prevalence rate is estimated at about 2.3 percent.

AIDS has flourished in sub-Saharan Africa for many reasons. Most of the countries of the region rank among the world's poorest. When the epidemic erupted, their weak medical

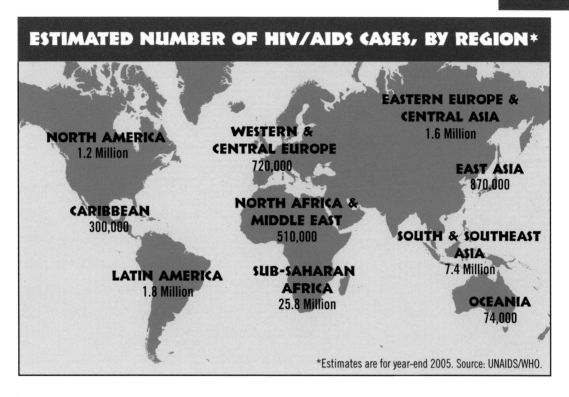

ESTIMATED NUMBER OF HIV/AIDS CASES, BY REGION*

EASTERN EUROPE & CENTRAL ASIA
1.6 Million

NORTH AMERICA
1.2 Million

WESTERN & CENTRAL EUROPE
720,000

EAST ASIA
870,000

CARIBBEAN
300,000

NORTH AFRICA & MIDDLE EAST
510,000

SOUTH & SOUTHEAST ASIA
7.4 Million

LATIN AMERICA
1.8 Million

SUB-SAHARAN AFRICA
25.8 Million

OCEANIA
74,000

*Estimates are for year-end 2005. Source: UNAIDS/WHO.

infrastructures (including a lack of medical facilities, equipment, and trained personnel) proved ineffective in containing it. In fact, in many cases, substandard practices at hospitals and clinics— such as the reuse of disposable plastic syringes and the failure to sterilize instruments—actually facilitated the transmission of HIV. In addition, few medical facilities had the blood testing equipment needed to diagnose HIV infections. As a result, many infected people did not know they had the disease and took no efforts to prevent spreading it to others. But even when HIV tests were available, many people were simply too poor to pay for them. Widespread ignorance of HIV status continues to hamper efforts to control AIDS in Africa, where about 90 percent of those who are HIV-positive do not know it.

Poverty has played a huge role in aiding the transmission of the disease among children and adults alike. Because they cannot afford bottled milk, poor HIV-positive mothers have breastfed their infants, transmitting the virus to their babies. Husbands have passed along HIV to wives because they had no money to pay for condoms. AIDS is also spread when the poor turn to prostitution in order to pay rent or buy food to survive.

STIGMA OF AIDS

Cultural attitudes have also contributed to the spread of HIV/AIDS in sub-Saharan Africa. Those living with AIDS are commonly shunned. Fearful of catching the disease, family members refuse to allow AIDS victims to live with them or share food. Landlords have been known to evict HIV-positive tenants. Husbands—who in many cases are responsible for infecting their wives—abandon them when they become ill. And in some sub-Saharan communities, a woman does not routinely inherit property upon the death of her husband, leaving her in desperate straits. In all of these cases, the ostracized and impoverished are more likely to be pushed into trading sex for necessities to survive.

Because of the stigma attached to the disease, many men will not take tests to find out if they are infected with the AIDS virus. Yet they remain sexually active and, if they are carrying HIV, spread the infection to others—often younger, poorer women. Some men do not accept the possibility that they could have HIV, and they refuse to use condoms to prevent spreading the disease.

For the middle-class African male, admission of being HIV-positive means losing status, friends, and possibilities for promotion. Many public figures in Africa who have AIDS never acknowledge that fact. Their obituaries often state that they died "after a long illness" or attribute death to other causes. Because of the stigma of AIDS, families do not want the true cause of death to be known.

However, in 2005 one grieving public figure spoke up. In January of that year, former South African president and anti-AIDS activist Nelson Mandela announced that his 54-year-old son had died from AIDS. During the course of Makgatho L.

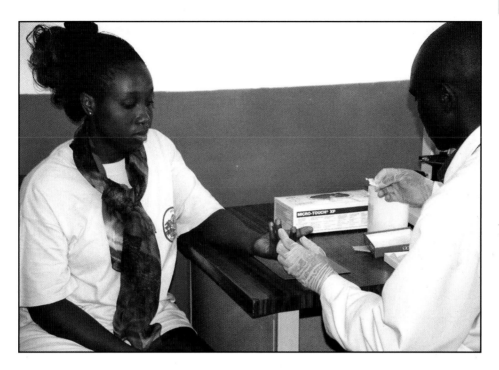

A simple blood test can screen for HIV. But in many African countries, people at risk refuse to get tested, in large part because of the stigma of being HIV-positive.

Mandela's illness, his family had kept quiet about its cause. However, on the day of his death, his father revealed the truth at a news conference in Johannesburg, South Africa. Nelson Mandela stated that Africans needed to break the taboo about AIDS, because keeping the illness a secret implied it was shameful: "That is why I have announced that my son has died of AIDS," he said. "Let us give publicity to H.I.V./AIDS and not hide it, because the only way to make it appear like a normal illness like TB, like cancer, is always to come out and say somebody has died because of H.I.V./AIDS, and people will stop regarding it as something extraordinary."

WOMEN AND AIDS

In Africa almost 6 in 10 (57 percent) of the HIV-positive adults are women. Among young people ages 15 to 24, three-fourths of those with HIV are female. In many cases women and girls have

Nelson Mandela drops a yellow rose on the casket of his son Makgatho, January 15, 2005. Earlier the former president of South Africa had revealed the cause of his 54-year-old son's death as AIDS, breaking a taboo against publicly discussing the disease.

no knowledge of how HIV is transmitted and ways to prevent infection. But even when they are educated about AIDS, African women live in a culture of gender inequality. They often play a subordinate role in their society and risk abuse if they refuse sexual relations or ask that their husband use a condom.

AIDS PROGRAMS

Since the mid-1980s, governments and international organizations, including the World Health Organization and many NGOs, have worked together to establish AIDS education programs in an effort to slow the spread of the disease. Anti-AIDS programs seek to provide clear and accurate information about HIV/AIDS and to dispel myths, prejudices, and fears.

Efforts to educate people include high school HIV-prevention clubs (every high school in Ethiopia has one) and billboards and posters promoting the use of condoms during sexual activity as a means to prevent transmission of the human immunodeficiency virus. Many of these government-sponsored programs promote following the "ABCs" of prevention: abstinence, being faithful, and condom use.

Some prevention programs provide HIV testing services, as well as counseling to educate infected patients on how to avoid passing the disease along to others. Other AIDS programs include monitoring and antiretroviral treatment of patients. Researchers have found that antiretroviral treatment reduces the amount of HIV in the blood, which lowers the probability of spreading the virus to others.

Still other AIDS programs focus on alleviating the social disruption that the disease has inflicted. These programs might, for example, provide counseling and support for the spouses and orphaned children of AIDS victims.

GOVERNMENT ROLE IN HIV PREVALENCE

The Republic of South Africa, although one of Africa's more prosperous nations, has one of the highest HIV infection rates on the continent. About 5 million South Africans in the 15–49 age group, or more than one in five, have AIDS or are infected with HIV.

Some people believe the South African government bears significant blame for these high numbers. For several years, the

A banner kicking off a condom-promotion campaign in Sierra Leone. Condom use is one of the so-called ABCs of HIV prevention, but the virus continues to spread through unprotected sex.

administration of South African president Thabo Mbeki, who was first elected in 1999, questioned the existence of a link between HIV and AIDS. Despite the availability of free anti-retroviral drugs, his government refused to sponsor a national prevention program for infants. Mbeki's administration also failed to provide antiretroviral drugs for HIV-positive South Africans who could not afford them. It was not until March 2003 that the government began backing efforts to provide anti-retrovirals to HIV-positive South Africans.

In stark contrast, the political leaders of Uganda, including President Yoweri Museveni, took a strong stand against AIDS. Although Uganda was among the first African countries in which AIDS appeared, and although its HIV adult prevalence rate reached about 18 percent by 1992, by 2003 the rate had fallen to an estimated 4.1 percent. One reason for Uganda's success in reducing its national HIV infection rate, some observers say, is that the Ugandan president broke religious and cultural taboos by speaking openly about AIDS.

Studies show that 99 percent of Ugandan adults are aware of the dangers of AIDS and of ways to prevent infection. They have gained much of this information from government-sponsored campaigns to raise awareness of the epidemic.

Africa contains more than 50 countries and a multitude of cultures. As the cases of Uganda and South Africa indicate, national responses to the AIDS epidemic have varied in their approaches—and in their effectiveness. However, it is clear that to defeat the disease, all nations need effective prevention programs, access to treatment, and supportive funding.

INTERNATIONAL INVOLVEMENT

Although AIDS was identified in Africa in the early 1980s, in the decade that followed only limited efforts addressed the growing epidemic within the continent. Many policymakers did not recognize the potential impact of the disease. Contributions to anti-AIDS programs in Africa were small, consisting of donations of millions of dollars when billions were needed to make any headway against the growing epidemic.

In 1996 the UN established the Joint United Nations Program on HIV/AIDS (UNAIDS) to help bring together and coordinate efforts to address the HIV/AIDS epidemic around the world. Based in Geneva, Switzerland, UNAIDS includes representation from 10 separate UN agencies. Its programs work to prevent transmission of AIDS and provide care and support to infected individuals. UNAIDS also works in partnerships with national and local governments, NGOs, and the private sector in the development and implementation of AIDS education programs.

The Global AIDS Program (GAP) is an independent public-private partnership that includes the American Red Cross and the U.S. Centers for Disease Control and Prevention. Largely funded by the U.S. government and by charitable organizations such as the Bill & Melinda Gates Foundation, GAP works to put HIV/AIDS projects into operation in Africa. Various initiatives focus on HIV prevention, care and support for people living with HIV, and support for children orphaned by AIDS.

Although funding to fight the global HIV/AIDS pandemic was low at first, contributions began to increase as governments, businesses, and individuals around the world became aware of the scope of the AIDS problem. According to a 2004 UNAIDS survey, in 73 low- and middle-income countries, global funding for the fight against AIDS increased from $2.1 billion in 2001 to $6.1 billion in 2004.

Still, experts believe that much more money is needed, especially as the number of people with HIV continues to increase. Some AIDS analysts believe that $15 billion will be needed in 2007 and that $25 billion will be required by 2015.

A United Nations General Assembly meeting on HIV/AIDS. In 2000 the UN's member states committed themselves to halting, and beginning to reverse, the spread of HIV within 15 years. By 2005, however, prospects for achieving this objective of the UN Millennium Development Goals already appeared to be dimming, as key targets were missed. In sub-Saharan Africa the UN reported no progress in the fight to contain the AIDS virus.

PRESIDENT'S EMERGENCY PLAN FOR AIDS RELIEF

In January 2003 U.S. president George W. Bush announced the establishment of a U.S. government fund to combat AIDS in developing countries. He promised to back this effort with a U.S. contribution of $15 billion over a five-year period. Called the President's Emergency Plan for AIDS Relief, or PEPFAR, the fund set a target to bring life-extending drug treatments to at least 2 million people.

In May 2003 the U.S. Congress approved PEPFAR, with the stipulation that 55 percent of the funding be allocated for HIV/AIDS treatment (primarily the purchase and distribution of antiretroviral medication), 15 percent to the care of those with AIDS or HIV, 20 percent for HIV/AIDS prevention, and 10 percent for helping orphans. By 2005 PEPFAR was focused primarily on fighting AIDS in a dozen African countries, along with Haiti, Guyana, and Vietnam.

AFFORDABLE
AND AVAILABLE DRUGS

One of the biggest problems in defeating AIDS in Africa has been the difficulty of making high-cost medications available to those infected with HIV. The pharmaceutical companies that make and own the patents to antiretroviral therapy drugs price them high enough to cover research and development costs and to make a profit before the patents expire. However, the typical person in a developing country cannot afford to pay several thousand dollars per year for these medications.

When ARVs first became available, African governments that wished to provide them to their citizens at subsidized costs could not afford the high prices either. To bring down costs, they turned to generic drug manufacturers in South Africa, India, Brazil, Thailand, and China that were producing less expensive copies of patented ARV drugs. In 2000 the United States rebuked several countries, including South Africa and Zimbabwe, for violating pharmaceutical company patents by using generic versions of anti-AIDS drugs. Several major pharmaceutical companies threatened lawsuits.

In response, Médicins Sans Frontières and other organizations initiated media campaigns to publicize the issue. Providing antiretroviral treatment for HIV patients, they pointed out, not only extended the lives of those already infected but also dramatically lowered rates of new infections. Thus any realistic strategy to stop the AIDS epidemic would have to include the provision of adequate supplies of ARV drugs to developing countries, at prices these countries could afford.

Eventually the pharmaceutical companies agreed to cut their prices in these markets. Some began providing donated medications as well. However, American-funded anti-AIDS programs, particularly the $15 billion PEPFAR initiative, continued to stipulate that their funds could not be used to purchase generic drugs because of violations of pharmaceutical manufacturers' patents. Generic drugs also had to be approved by the U.S. Food and Drug Administration (FDA) before they could be purchased with money donated by the U.S. government.

This last barrier was lifted in January 2005, when the FDA officially approved the use of generic drugs manufactured by a South African firm producing an AZT and lamivudine combination (the equivalent of GlaxoSmithKline's drug Combivir). It is packaged in a plastic blister with another pill, nevirapine (the equivalent of Viramune, by Boehringer-Ingel). The brand-name manufacturers had given approval for their patented drugs to be made in generic versions. FDA approval meant that developing nations benefiting from President Bush's AIDS funding initiative could now buy generic drugs instead of the more expensive brand-name versions, and the cost savings would allow treatment of two or three times as many HIV-positive patients as had been possible previously.

Patent violations remain an issue with single-pill ARV therapy. Some generic drug manufacturers have combined three antiretroviral drugs normally produced by two different pharmaceutical companies into one pill. As of mid-2005, AIDS programs funded by the U.S. government were not allowed to purchase this form of ARV medication, as brand-name pharmaceutical companies cited concerns both about its safety and potential patent violations. However, some groups believe that the low cost and ease of use of a single-pill, combination drug therapy make it a valuable contribution to the fight against AIDS in poor countries.

REACHING "3 BY 5"

In December 2003 the World Health Organization set a goal of "3 by 5" for treating HIV/AIDS in developing countries. The WHO

Demonstrators in Nairobi, Kenya, demand access to AIDS treatments, September 2003. The high cost of antiretroviral drugs — which are effective in reducing the amount of HIV in the bloodstream and thus delaying the progression of disease — long stood in the way of their widespread use in impoverished African nations. Recently, however, pharmaceutical companies have agreed to reduce prices for their antiretroviral drugs, and to permit the manufacture of generic versions, for developing nations.

goal directed HIV/AIDS programs to work to deliver antiretroviral drugs to 3 million people in the developing world by the end of 2005. At the time this target was set, fewer than 300,000 people in developing nations were receiving these anti-AIDS drugs.

Despite a strong effort, the goal was not met, although some progress was made. In June 2004 a WHO report said that the number of people in developing nations who were receiving ARVs had increased to 440,000. And by June 2005 that number stood at approximately 1 million. Almost half were receiving drugs that had been sold at deeply discounted prices by major pharmaceutical companies; the rest were taking generic antiretrovirals.

THE SPREAD OF HIV IN AFRICA

ADULT PREVALENCE RATE, 1986

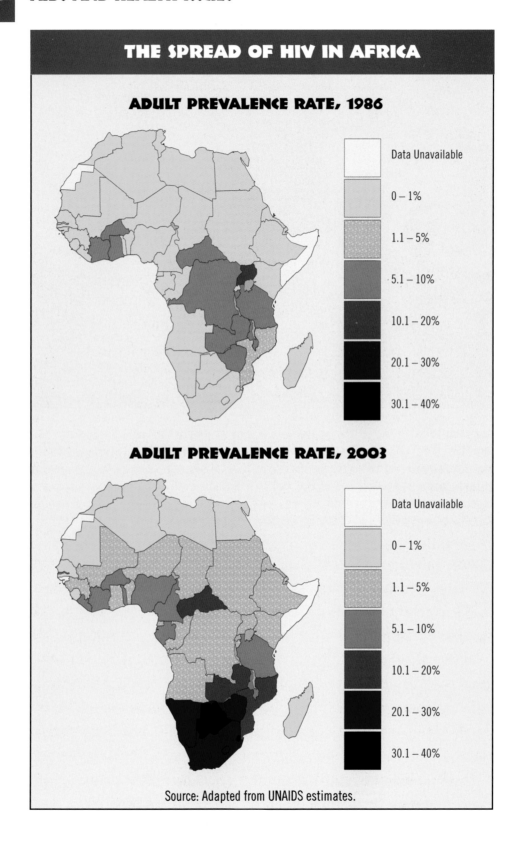

Data Unavailable

0 – 1%

1.1 – 5%

5.1 – 10%

10.1 – 20%

20.1 – 30%

30.1 – 40%

ADULT PREVALENCE RATE, 2003

Data Unavailable

0 – 1%

1.1 – 5%

5.1 – 10%

10.1 – 20%

20.1 – 30%

30.1 – 40%

Source: Adapted from UNAIDS estimates.

Although the "3 by 5" initiative benefited from immense effort and significant funding, it encountered obstacles such as a short supply of the combination therapy pills and a lack of trained staff to deliver care. Still, by the end of 2005, at least 700,000 more people in developing countries were receiving ARV treatment than had been the case just two years earlier.

VACCINES AND MICROBICIDES

While ARVs can extend the lives of the HIV-positive and reduce transmission of the virus, a vaccine may be the only way to eradicate AIDS. Vaccine development efforts are currently under way in several quarters. The Harvard School of Public Health's AIDS Initiative is focusing on development of a vaccine against HIV-1C, which is most common in Africa, by using genetic material from the virus strain. Other researchers are trying to develop therapeutic vaccines, which would treat people already infected.

Before a vaccine can be used with the general population, it must go through three phases of clinical trials, or testing, to ensure its safety. Collaborations among the government of Botswana and several local, regional, and international institutions and organizations are establishing ways to conduct vaccine trials in that country.

Several pharmaceutical companies and research organizations have been pursuing the development of an HIV/AIDS vaccine under the support and direction of the Global HIV/AIDS Vaccine Enterprise. This group has adopted a multipronged strategy, sponsoring efforts such as the use of alternative scientific approaches, the funding of additional clinical trials, and the training of researchers in countries where AIDS is endemic. Much of the organization's work is funded by the Bill & Melinda Gates Foundation.

Experts believe that the creation of a safe and effective AIDS vaccine, which presents extremely complex scientific problems,

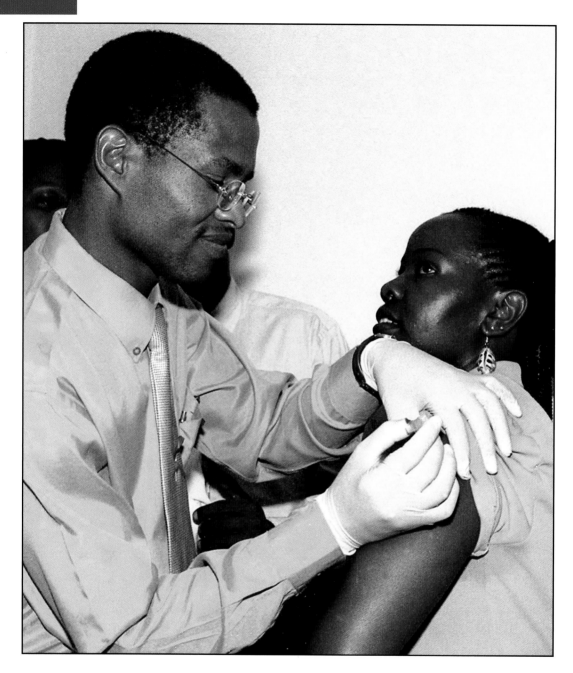

Pamela Mandela, a Kenyan physician, receives an experimental HIV vaccine developed under the aegis of the International AIDS Vaccine Initiative (IAVI), March 2001. Although results from the clinical trial in which Mandela participated ultimately proved disappointing, the search for a vaccine against HIV continues.

will require billions of dollars. One has study estimated annual research costs for AIDS vaccines at approximately $682 million.

Other anti-HIV research has focused on the development of microbicides that kill HIV. Such compounds could be used by women intravaginally to protect themselves from HIV transmission during sexual activity. Experimental versions in gel form exist, but they have not yet proven effective against HIV.

MALARIA AND TUBERCULOSIS

The infectious diseases malaria and tuberculosis (TB) are the second and third leading causes of death, respectively, in Africa. Unlike AIDS, which is relatively new, these two illnesses have plagued humans for centuries.

MALARIA

The second-deadliest disease of sub-Saharan Africa, malaria ranks as the world's most severe tropical parasitic disease. Worldwide, there are some 300 million to 500 million cases of malaria each year, with 1 million to 2 million fatalities. About 90 percent of all deaths from malaria occur in sub-Saharan Africa. Children under the age of five are particularly vulnerable. The World Health Organization estimates that malaria kills a child in Africa every 30 seconds; the disease claims the lives of many more African children than either HIV/AIDS or tuberculosis. If children do not receive prompt treatment after developing malaria symptoms, they usually die within 72 hours.

(Opposite) A mother tries to comfort her five-year-old son, who lays stricken with a severe case of malaria, El Geneina, Sudan. Debilitating and often deadly, malaria attacks as many as 500 million people from tropical regions of the world each year, killing 1 million to 2 million. The vast majority of victims live in sub-Saharan Africa.

In certain parts of sub-Saharan Africa, malaria occurs and recurs frequently. *World Malaria Report 2005*, produced by the World Health Organization and UNICEF, notes endemic areas where one of every two people contracts the disease each year. In those areas, malaria has taken an especially devastating toll in lives, as well as in costs for medical care and lost productivity. And the number of cases of the disease continues to rise in sub-Saharan Africa, where malaria killed twice as many people in 2000 as it did in 1990.

CAUSE, SYMPTOMS, AND DIAGNOSIS

A deadly disease throughout the world for many centuries, malaria was once thought to be caused by bad air, and was so named: *mal*, meaning "bad," and *aria*, meaning "air." In 1880 the French

Charles Louis Alphonse Laveran, photographed around 1900. The French physician correctly identified *Plasmodia*, microscopic protozoan parasites, as the cause of malaria.

physician Charles Louis Alphonse Laveran discovered that the disease is actually caused by a microscopic single-celled parasite, or protozoan, carried by the *Anopheles* mosquito. Malaria is common in tropical and subtropical regions of Africa, where this mosquito thrives in the warm climate. The malaria-causing protozoa, called *Plasmodia*, damage the human body by attacking and destroying the red blood cells (which carry oxygen).

Four different species of *Plasmodia* can cause malaria, but the species common to sub-Saharan Africa is the most lethal. Called *Plasmodium falciparum*, it accounts for more than 70 percent of malaria infections in Africa.

The mosquito becomes a malaria carrier when it bites and takes blood from someone already infected with the disease. After about two weeks, the protozoa will have reproduced and migrated from the mosquito's gut to its salivary glands, making the insect infectious whenever it bites again. When the mosquito takes its next meal, the bite transmits the protozoa into the bloodstream of the new victim, or host.

Once in the human body, *Plasmodia* parasites travel to the liver and reproduce within the red blood cells. Malarial attacks occur when the rapidly reproducing parasites become so numerous that they cause the cells to rupture, releasing more parasites into the bloodstream to attack more red blood cells. Each time the red cells rupture, the victim suffers from a high fever. In an attempt to lower the high temperature, the body sweats profusely—until the next malarial attack and subsequent fever.

Intermittent fevers lasting two or more hours each are characteristic of malaria. In malaria caused by *Plasmodium falciparum*, fevers recur every 48 hours. Most victims will die from the infection if not treated.

In certain parts of tropical Africa, the malaria parasite is present in the entire population, although for most of the time the hosts do not exhibit symptoms of the disease. However, they tend to have anemia (a low number of red blood cells), weakness, and swelling of the spleen.

Symptoms of malaria include attacks of shaking and chills, followed by a high fever that may reach 106°F (41°C) and severe headache. These symptoms may be accompanied by nausea, muscular pain, and other flu-like symptoms. When malaria is not treated within a day or two of the onset of symptoms, the body is soon starved of oxygen because of the continuing loss of red blood cells. Convulsions, coma, and death soon follow.

Because malaria causes severe anemia in pregnant women, the disease contributes to maternal deaths in malaria-prone regions of Africa. The disease also impairs the physical and intellectual development of children who manage to survive. Children who have battled numerous episodes of malaria have been known to suffer from chronic anemia, weakness, and stunted development.

TREATMENT AND PREVENTION

Malaria is a curable disease if promptly diagnosed and adequately treated. Effective treatments were first developed in 1820, when quinine was isolated from the bark of the cinchona tree (native to Peru). Chloroquine eventually became the standard antimalarial treatment.

Since the 1990s, however, *Plasmodium falciparum* has become resistant to chloroquine and another commonly used drug, sulphadoxinepyrimethamine. A more effective—and also more expensive—treatment relies on artemisinin, which is derived from the Chinese herb *Artemisia annua* (also referred to as qinghaosu or sweet wormwood). When combined with other antimalarial drugs, artemisinin-based combination therapies have proved very effective against *P. falciparum* malaria in many parts of sub-Saharan Africa. However, drugs derived from *Artemisia annua* are hard to produce, and health workers complain of scarce supplies and difficulties in delivering and administering these drugs to at-risk populations.

There are numerous ways to prevent the spread of malaria. Many drugs used to treat the disease can also provide protection against infection—and if fewer people have been sickened by malaria, mosquitoes have fewer infectious sources from which to transmit the disease.

Malaria can also be prevented by eliminating the mosquito population wherever the disease is endemic. During the 1950s and 1960s, WHO workers successfully eradicated or controlled malaria in many parts of the world by spraying the interior walls of homes (since that is where the mosquito rests after eating) with the insecticide DDT (dichlorodiphenyltrichloroethane) and other inexpensive pesticides. The synthetic chemical DDT proved very effective in wiping out the mosquito populations, but its use became controversial because it can have adverse effects on the environment. (Legislators banned the insecticide in the United States in the 1970s, but it is approved by the World Health Organization for killing disease-carrying insects.)

Large-scale insecticidal spraying programs did not occur in Africa until the 1990s, and they have not been as successful as in other parts of the world. One problem is that in regions where frequent applications of DDT were used, the *Anopheles* mosquito has become resistant to the pesticide. Such spraying programs can also be very expensive when the pesticides must be transported to remote areas and reapplied frequently.

Environmental management techniques are another strategy for controlling the mosquito populations. Such techniques include draining or spraying stagnant bodies of water where the insects breed.

A seldom-used, but very effective, method of preventing malarial infection in Africa is the use of insecticide-treated mosquito netting to cover individuals when sleeping. However, chemically treated bed nets cost $2 to $5 apiece, which is a price beyond the means of most sub-Saharan households. As a result, fewer than 2 percent of Africans use them.

As part of a government antimalaria campaign, chemically treated bed nets are distributed to residents of a Uganda town.

ERADICATING MALARIA

Malaria has spread in Africa as the range of the *Anopheles* mosquito has expanded and its populations have increased. Changing patterns of temperature and rainfall (which some researchers attribute to global warming) have allowed the insects to move into parts of Africa, such as the highlands of East Africa, where they had previously been unable to survive.

In the 1990s the World Health Organization, UNICEF, the U.S. Agency for International Development (USAID), and other organizations began a concerted effort to eradicate malaria in Africa by using three strategies: ensuring antimalarial drug treatment within 24 hours of fever onset, supplying insecticide-treated bed nets and spraying homes, and providing drugs for pregnant women, who would pass along immunity to their newborns during the first months of life.

In April 2000, representatives from 44 African countries met in Abuja, Nigeria, to discuss the problem of malaria in Africa. The resulting Abuja Declaration, signed by more than 20 African heads of state, committed the countries to devote at least 15 percent of their annual budgets to the public health sector to fight malaria. It also called on international aid donors to contribute at least $1 billion to the cause. Subsequent yearly meetings of African leaders continue to address the need to prevent and control malaria and other deadly diseases in Africa.

One initiative targeting malaria is the Roll Back Malaria (RBM) Partnership, launched in 1998, which has set the goal of halving the number of malaria cases by 2010 (by reducing it from more than 1 million to 500,000). It combines the efforts of 90 partners, including four UN agencies (the United Nations Development Program, UNICEF, the WHO, and the World Bank).

Until recently, funding for this initiative was low. A March 2003 study showed that from 1998 to 2002, donations for the program amounted to about $100 million per year, far short of the $1.5 billion to $2.5 billion necessary for RBM to meet its goal.

In July 2005, on the eve of the G8 summit in Scotland, the Bush administration promised to strengthen the U.S. commitment to fighting malaria in Africa. President Bush announced that $1.2 billion (of a $1.7 billion U.S. aid package to Africa) would be spent over five years for antimalaria efforts. Initially, the aid would be directed to Tanzania, Uganda, and Angola, but coverage was expected eventually to include at least 15 other African countries.

The Malaria Vaccines Initiative and the Medicines for Malaria Venture are two public-private partnerships that include collaboration by the World Health Organization, the World Bank, various foundations, and industry. Both initiatives have received significant support from the Bill & Melinda Gates Foundation, which contributed a five-year, $168 million grant in September 2003 to speed the search for drug-related solutions to malaria.

In October 2004 the Gates Foundation and the pharmaceutical company GlaxoSmithKline reported partial success in the development of a malaria vaccine. The vaccine reportedly reduced the risk of infection by 30 percent and the severity of infections by more than 50 percent. However, more years of development are needed before possible release on the market.

Additional drug development and antimalaria research projects are being sponsored by universities, governments, and pharmaceutical manufacturers (including Sanofi-Aventis SA, Pfizer, and Novartis AG).

TUBERCULOSIS

Once referred to as "consumption," tuberculosis is a disease caused by a bacterium, *Mycobacterium tuberculosis* (or the tubercle bacillus), that attacks and grows in the lungs and throat. TB has existed for millennia; evidence of infection has been found on 7,000-year-old skeletons and in Egyptian mummies. During the 17th and 18th centuries tuberculosis killed one in five adults. By the 19th century it had become even more lethal, causing one in three deaths.

Today, according to Médicins Sans Frontières, 8 million people develop active cases of tuberculosis annually, and the disease claims 2 million lives each year. Many other people are infected but do not show symptoms. In fact, the World Health Organization estimates that approximately one-third of the world's population is currently infected with the TB bacillus. The WHO predicts that nearly 1 billion people worldwide will be infected between 2000 and 2020 if efforts to stop its spread prove unsuccessful.

Weakened by tuberculosis and malnutrition, a farmer in Zambia rests in his parched field. Over the past 15 years, the number of TB cases in Africa has exploded, mostly because of the AIDS pandemic.

While the number of tuberculosis cases has dropped throughout much of the developed world, TB cases have been increasing at an alarming pace in Africa. According to USAID, the number of diagnosed cases of TB in Africa more than doubled over a 13-year period—from 200,000 in 1990 to 539,000 in 2003.

The major resurgence of tuberculosis in Africa can be attributed to the AIDS pandemic, as TB is the most frequent opportunistic infection associated with AIDS in Africa. In fact, individuals with HIV are 50 times more likely to develop TB in a given year than are people not infected with HIV. TB is also the leading killer of those afflicted by HIV/AIDS; about 35 percent of AIDS deaths result from opportunistic infections of tuberculosis.

Worldwide, approximately 12 million people have been infected by both HIV and TB. Most of them (approximately two-thirds) can be found in sub-Saharan Africa. Nigeria has the highest number of newly diagnosed cases per year.

CAUSE, SYMPTOMS, AND DIAGNOSIS

Mycobacterium tuberculosis is easily passed from person to person by the sneeze or cough of infected individuals. Once the droplets of moisture containing the bacteria are inhaled, they infect the lungs, causing the formation of hard swellings called tubercles in the air sacs, or alveoli (where oxygen is absorbed from the lung into the bloodstream).

During this initial infection, symptoms such as fever, rash, or nausea may occur. In some cases, the tubercle infections may remain dormant in the lungs for several years. However, in infants, children, the elderly, and individuals with compromised immune systems, a second tuberculosis infection soon follows. The tubercles rupture, releasing the tuberculosis bacteria, which are carried to other parts of the lung, to the lymphatic system, and to the blood. The TB bacteria can eventually infect many parts of the body, including the bones, brain, joints, kidneys, and skin.

When the bacteria primarily affect the lungs, the disease is called pulmonary tuberculosis. Victims of pulmonary tuberculosis suffer from

A vial of sputum coughed up by a TB victim. The blood in the sample indicates that the disease has significantly damaged the blood vessels in the patient's lungs.

frequent coughing that brings up mucus and—when the blood vessels in the lungs become damaged—blood. Additional symptoms include chest pain, fatigue, weight loss, chills, fever, and night sweats. TB usually does not kill its victims quickly, but is a long-term wasting disease.

In industrialized nations, several kinds of tests exist to diagnose tuberculosis. Skin tests will show whether the bacillus is in the body, X rays can reveal the presence of tubercles, and lab tests can be used to diagnose the presence of the bacteria. These latter tests involve examining a sample of sputum (spit) under a microscope in order to determine the presence of *Mycobacterium tuberculosis*. However, patients may have the disease even when they test negative.

TREATMENT

Most of the drugs used to treat TB date from the 1940s, and they require a six-month course to effect a cure. Some therapy regimens may require up to two years of treatment before a person is completely cured. Among the most effective anti-TB drugs are isoniazid, rifampin, rifapentine, ethambutol, streptomycin, and pyrazinamide. These drugs prevent bacteria from reproducing within the body and help the immune system fight the disease.

In some parts of the world, including Africa, tuberculosis has become resistant to standard therapies. That is, the commonly used treatments no longer cure TB. Such drug resistance occurs when people do not take the full course of therapy, which allows some bacteria to survive and mutate. As a result, physicians now often give medications in combinations of two or more drugs in order to ensure their effectiveness.

To cure tuberculosis patients and avoid drug resistance, the World Health Organization advocates that governments adopt a strategy called DOTS (Directly Observed Therapy Short course). DOTS requires, among other things, standardized treatment for

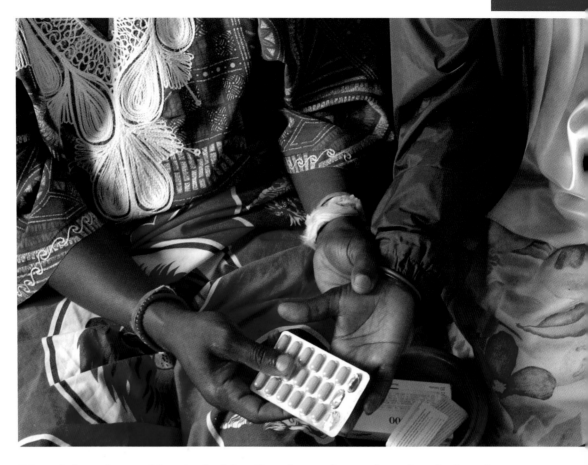

Tuberculosis can be cured, but standard drug therapies require a strict regimen lasting at least six months. When patients fail to complete their course of treatment—as has happened frequently in Africa—drug-resistant strains of the bacteria that cause TB can emerge. To prevent this, African governments have started to employ a strategy known as DOTS, by which a health worker directly observes patients as they take their daily medication. This photo shows the strategy in action in South Africa.

all TB patients, an uninterrupted supply of the necessary drugs, and well-staffed clinics and monitoring systems. An indispensable part of the program is observation of the patient by a health care worker or family member who ensures that each dose of medicine is taken and that the entire six-month course of treatment is completed.

For the most part, the DOTS strategy has proved quite successful in developing countries, where it has produced an average cure rate of 80 percent. Unfortunately, in Africa many people do not have access to DOTS services. In Uganda, where the government advocates the DOTS strategy, more than half of the people with TB have not received such treatment because of inadequate health facilities. The government of South Africa makes use of the DOTS strategy as well, but only about half of that country's TB sufferers are served because there are not enough health workers for effective monitoring of patients and provision of treatment.

In remote or isolated parts of Africa, where the DOTS strategy cannot work, or in areas where it is not funded, other strategies may be used. For example, some anti-tuberculosis programs provide preventive therapy against the disease by giving the drug isoniazid to large numbers of at-risk people. Another method of controlling the spread of TB is to identify and treat tuberculosis carriers—people who have the disease without symptoms and without knowing they are infectious. Such carriers have caused TB outbreaks while remaining symptom-free themselves.

THE GLOBAL FUND TO FIGHT AIDS, TUBERCULOSIS AND MALARIA

In January 2002 the United Nations, led by Secretary-General Kofi Annan, launched an independent agency to focus efforts being made to combat three major diseases—which combined claim the lives of 10,000 Africans every day. The Global Fund to Fight AIDS, Tuberculosis and Malaria collects donations from governments, foundations, and individuals, and then channels money as grants into programs that battle these diseases in developing countries.

The Global Fund's largest donor countries are the United States (which made the founding contribution), France, Italy, and the Netherlands. Among private organizations, the biggest donor has been the Bill & Melinda Gates Foundation. As of

November 2005 the Global Fund had approved more than $4.4 billion in grant proposals and disbursed some $1.77 billion in grants for more than 300 programs in 127 countries. More than half (56 percent) of the grants awarded by the Global Fund as of November 2005 were designated for AIDS programs, with 31 percent allocated to antimalaria projects and 20 percent set aside for the fight against tuberculosis.

Reports from the Africa.com website in June 2005 indicated that some progress was being made in the fight against AIDS, TB, and malaria. Programs financed by the Global Fund had provided the means to expand treatment and services so that a total of 220,000 people were on AIDS antiretroviral treatment, 600,000 were being treated for TB under the DOTS strategy, and 1.55 million bed nets had been distributed or re-treated with chemicals to kill malaria-carrying mosquitoes.

4 DISEASES CAUSED BY LACK OF SAFE WATER

The World Health Organization estimates that at least one-sixth of the global population lacks access to safe water. In other words, more than 1 billion people live with water that is neither potable (safe to drink) nor suitable for sanitary needs. In most developing countries, more than half the people contract infectious diseases because of the lack of safe water and inadequate sanitation.

DIARRHEAL DISEASES

Some infectious diseases found in contaminated water attack the gastrointestinal tract, causing diarrhea. Severe diarrheal diseases can kill because they cause the body to dehydrate, or lose fluids. Infants, children, and the elderly, who have fewer fluid reserves in the body, are the most likely to fall victim to dehydration. Signs of such serious body fluid loss include strong thirst, little or no urine output, dry skin and mouth, sunken eyes, weakness, and rapid heart rate. Severe dehydration leads to chemical imbalances

(Opposite) At play in a stream of raw sewage, Nairobi, Kenya. Inadequate sanitation and a lack of access to potable water are responsible for a range of diseases, including cholera, dysentery, rotavirus, and schistosomiasis.

in the body, kidney failure, coma, and death.

Worldwide, diarrheal diseases account for 2 million to 6 million deaths each year, with 90 percent of the victims consisting of children under the age of five. Diarrheal diseases occur frequently: on average, the children in developing countries suffer 12 episodes per year. Among the most serious diarrheal diseases in Africa are cholera, dysentery, and rotavirus.

CHOLERA

A major pathogen that causes diarrheal disease is the bacterium *Vibro cholerae*, which causes cholera, an acute intestinal infection. Cholera is spread when

people consume water or food that has been contaminated with infected solid body waste, or feces. Unsanitary conditions affecting a community's water supply can lead to outbreaks of the disease.

Once inside the intestines, the cholera bacteria multiply rapidly, releasing toxins that cause the body to produce large quantities of water and salts. Vomiting and leg cramps often accompany the resulting watery diarrhea. These symptoms of cholera occur one to three days after infection.

Health workers in Africa typically treat body fluid loss with water, sugar, and salts, given orally. Extreme dehydration may be treated with antibiotics, as well as fluids given intravenously (by IV). With proper treatment, cholera can be cured within a few days. In fact, the recovery can be dramatic, as Dr. Andrew Schechtman, a Médicins Sans Frontières volunteer working with cholera victims, describes in an MSF informational brochure:

> [W]ith a few hours' work you can essentially resurrect the dead. A patient arrives severely dehydrated, eyes sunken, skin loose on the bones, cold, pulseless, no blood pressure, non-responsive. We surround him, start an intravenous line (or two) and infuse six or seven liters of Ringer's solution (used in intravenous rehydration) over the next three hours. On my next pass through the cholera tent a few hours later, he will likely be sitting up asking for some food.

Although cholera is very treatable, getting medical care to regions where an outbreak has occurred can be difficult. If not treated, cholera can cause death in more than 50 percent of cases. The World Health Organization estimates that about 200,000 people in developing countries fall victim to the disease each year. It is prevalent in sub-Saharan regions, where in 2001 death rates reached as high as 30 percent of all reported cases. That year Africa reported 173,359 cases, or 94 percent of the world total. In September 2005 the United Nations reported that a cholera epidemic had affected tens of thousands of people living in West Africa, killing nearly 500.

Cholera is highly infectious. Preventing its spread requires aggressive treatment of all cases, the cleaning up of sources of contamination, and the establishment of good sanitation, as unsanitary conditions are a primary reason for outbreaks of the disease. Although a vaccine against cholera has been developed, it is not very effective; it provides only 25 to 50 percent immunity, and then only for a period of about six months.

The Liberian child in this photo is suffering from cholera, an intestinal infection that produces diarrhea and dehydration. Outbreaks of the illness occur where sanitation is lacking.

BACILLARY DYSENTERY, OR SHIGELLOSIS

Another serious disease that attacks the intestines is bacillary dysentery, which in Africa is commonly caused by the *Shigella* bacteria. These microbes are commonly found in water polluted with human feces. The bacteria can also be transmitted by food that has been contaminated by unwashed hands or by flies.

Once inside the body, the *Shigella* bacteria burrow into intestinal walls, causing severe inflammation of the large intestine. Symptoms of an infection include abdominal pain or cramps, vomiting, and severe diarrhea that may contain mucus and blood. *Shigella* dysentery, or shigellosis, also causes a sudden high fever. If not treated, victims of shigellosis usually recover within a few weeks, although death due to dehydration is possible. Treatment consists of antibiotics and replacement of lost body fluids and salts.

Records of shigellosis epidemics in sub-Saharan Africa date from the 1970s. Outbreaks typically occur in areas where people live in overcrowded conditions with poor sanitation, a common plight of refugees from political upheavals and natural disasters. In 1994 dysentery caused by an antibiotic-resistant strain of *Shigella* devastated refugee camps in Zaire (now the Democratic Republic of the Congo). In one month alone, dysentery killed 20,000 refugees from Rwanda who had fled to the camps because of civil war in their country.

Worldwide, there are almost 165 million cases of dysentery each year, with 163 million occurring in developing countries. About 60 percent of cases involve children who are younger than five years old. HIV-positive patients, who have compromised immune systems, are also quite vulnerable to *Shigella* dysentery. *Shigella* infections kill approximately 1 million people each year.

ROTAVIRUS

Rotavirus attacks the stomach as well as the intestines. Identified in the early 1970s, this waterborne virus can be particularly deadly in children aged six months to two years because it causes very rapid dehydration. The elderly and people with weak immune systems are also quite vulnerable. The most common cause of viral gastroenteritis (inflammation of the stomach and intestines) in the world, rotavirus causes severe diarrhea in 125 million children, and kills more than 600,000 of them, each year. Most of these victims live in developing countries.

The main symptoms of rotavirus are vomiting, diarrhea, fever, and stomach cramps, which can last four to six days. These symptoms occur 4 to 48 hours after infection. When rotavirus infection leads to untreated dehydration, coma and death quickly follow. Even when successfully treated, victims of the disease may become infected again. However, after a second infection, survivors will have enough antibodies in the blood to prevent further infection. Very young breastfed infants also receive antibodies against the disease from their mother's milk.

Rotavirus is highly contagious in areas with poor sanitation, as the virus is found in the feces of people who are infected. Contaminated food and drinking water also help spread the disease. Infection can be prevented with proper food handling and through hand washing. Researchers have developed a rotavirus vaccine that is 80 percent effective, but it requires further testing.

SCHISTOSOMIASIS

Also referred to as bilharzia, after the German physician Theodor Bilharz, who in 1851 identified the flatworm parasite that causes this disease, schistosomiasis is an intestinal and urinary tract infection. Although seldom fatal, the disease is debilitating,

Dangerous waters: The well at left is contaminated by animal waste, but residents of the northern Eritrean village of Ebremi do not have access to a safe source of water for their household needs.

causing long-term discomfort and chronic pain, and stunting the growth of children. The disease is second only to malaria as a public health problem in Africa.

The three species of the tiny parasitic worms, or schisto-somes, that cause this painful infection in Africa are *Schistosoma haematobium, Schistosoma mansoni*, and *Schistosoma intercalatum*. They spend part of their life cycle in freshwater snails, then travel from the water to the human body when people bathe, swim, or wade in water where the worms live.

The tiny schistosomes enter the human body through the skin and invade the bloodstream. The worms eventually end up in blood vessels near the bladder and intestines, where they reproduce and deposit eggs.

The first symptom of a schistosomiasis infection is an itchy rash that appears where the worms have penetrated the skin. A few weeks later, symptoms such as abdominal pain, coughing, fever, chills, muscle aches, and nausea occur. Blood appears in the urine if the disease is not treated. Severe infections cause damage to the liver, spleen, and intestines.

Sub-Saharan Africa contains about 85 percent of the world's 200 million schistosomiasis cases. Most are women and children, traditionally tasked with the job of collecting and hauling water for the household. They become infected while filling their containers when they wade or stand in water that has been infested with diseased snails.

Schistosomiasis is prevalent in Egypt in the region around the Aswan High Dam, which controls the floodwaters of the Nile River. Built in southeastern Egypt to provide year-round irrigation, the Aswan High Dam has been blamed for increasing the number of cases of schistosomiasis in the Nile Valley and Nile Delta area. The constant presence of water in irrigation canals prevents the snail population from dying off, so the parasitic worms have thrived in the area, and the disease has spread.

Lake Nasser, one of the world's largest man-made reservoirs, can be seen behind the Aswan High Dam in this satellite photo. Completed in 1970, the Aswan High Dam has tamed the Nile River's annual flooding and provided irrigation water for agriculture in Egypt, but it has also been blamed for increasing the number of schistosomiasis cases in the region.

Other countries whose populations suffer from severe intestinal schistosomiasis are Mauritania and Senegal; there the Diama Dam and others on the Senegal River contribute to snail infestations. Many freshwater lakes in Africa, such as Lake Malawi, also harbor bilharzia.

Schistosomiasis is treated with the drug praziquantel, which must be given over the course of six months. With proper care, there is little likelihood of death from schistosomiasis. However, some drug-resistant parasites have evolved because of patient noncompliance with the extended course of treatment. Ways to prevent schistosomiasis include educating at-risk populations about how infection occurs, improving sanitation, and removing the disease-carrying snails from lakes, rivers, canals, and other bodies of water used by people.

According to WHO estimates, 1.8 million cases of schistosomiasis occurred in Africa in 2002, with 15,000 deaths attributed to the disease. Some researchers believe that schistosomiasis has a much higher death rate, but because it is a chronic condition, exact numbers are difficult to determine.

TRACHOMA

A highly contagious, chronic inflammation of the mucous membranes of the eyes, trachoma is caused by a form of the *Chlamydia trachomatis* bacterium. The disease is prevalent in parts of Africa where there is not enough water for people to wash their faces and hands regularly. In these conditions, bacteria found in discharge from the eyes and in mucus from the noses of infected individuals are spread by unwashed hands or by contact with contaminated towels or cloths used to wipe the face. Research has also shown that the *Chlamydia* bacterium is transmitted by *Musca sorbens*, a fly that is attracted to the eyes.

Symptoms of trachoma, which is a leading cause of blindness in Africa, occur about a week after infection. Like conjunctivitis, trachoma causes swelling of the eyelids, pain, discharge, and sensitivity to light. However, unlike conjunctivitis, the *Chlamydia trachomatis* infection may last for several years, or recur so often that it causes scarring of the conjunctiva (the clear mucous membrane lining the inside of the eyelid and the white part of the eye). In this extremely painful, advanced stage of the disease, called trichiasis, the eyelashes turn inward, scraping the corneas of the eyes and eventually causing blindness.

Treatment of trachoma entails a four-to-six-week course of antibiotics such as tetracycline, erythromycin, or sulfonamides. With prompt medical therapy, victims of trachoma can achieve full recovery. Surgery is required in treating trichiasis.

Trachoma can be prevented by practicing good hygiene and by improving the water supply and sanitation facilities. According to the World Health Organization, having a liter a day of clean water for hand washing can prevent trachoma infection. However, few people living in drought-stricken regions of Africa have access to water for this purpose.

Trachoma is found mostly in Africa and the Middle East. It causes one-third of the cases of blindness in Ethiopia (which is estimated to have the highest amount of blindness in the world). Researchers have found that, in the West African country of Niger, 44 percent of children under the age of 10 suffer from trachoma. Worldwide, the disease affects about 150 million people.

TYPHOID FEVER

The bacterium *Salmonella enterica* serotype typhi causes typhoid fever, a life-threatening illness characterized by high fever, weakness, severe headache, nausea, and sometimes diarrhea. The bacteria are spread through infected water or food.

Worldwide, there are approximately 12 million to 17 million cases of typhoid fever, and about 600,000 people die from the disease, each year. Typhoid fever epidemics occur mostly in

Children in a Tanzanian village wait their turn to be screened for signs of trachoma, a highly contagious condition that, left untreated, can cause blindness. Trachoma occurs where people have insufficient supplies of water for proper hygiene.

developing countries, which often have water supplies contaminated with human wastes.

The *Salmonella typhi* bacterium is spread by seemingly healthy carriers, as well as by those who exhibit symptoms of the disease. The bacteria are shed in the body wastes (feces and urine), and are passed along when an individual drinks water or eats food contaminated by *S. typhi*.

One to three weeks after infection with the typhoid bacteria, the victim develops symptoms. A fever, accompanied by headaches and abdominal pain, occurs during the first week of the disease. During the second week, the fever peaks, and the patient becomes weak and sometimes delirious. Red spots may appear on the chest and abdomen. Diarrhea follows during the third week, and symptoms begin to clear by the fourth.

Typhoid fever can cause death when the bacteria create holes in the intestinal wall and the contents of the intestines leak into the abdomen, resulting in abdominal infections. In other cases, the bacteria cause intestinal bleeding that also can be fatal.

Treatment with antibiotic drugs stops the growth of *S. typhi* and helps speed recovery for the patient. Good hygiene and public sanitation are effective in preventing the spread of typhoid fever. Although a vaccine made from killed typhoid fever bacteria exists, few people in Africa have access to it.

PROVIDING SAFE WATER

In much of Africa, clean drinking water and sanitary facilities—basics that residents of industrialized nations take for granted—do not exist. More than half of Africa's people lack access to safe water. Often, the only water source for rural villagers is a spring located several miles away that has been contaminated by human and animal waste.

Among the countries with the least access to safe water are Tanzania, Nigeria, and Ethiopia. In fact, most illnesses in Ethiopia are due to water-related diseases: 75 percent of the people in that country lack potable water and 85 percent do not have basic sanitation.

A woman fills her water jug from a pump near Alem Kitmama, Ethiopia. For people in the developed world, getting the water needed for drinking, cooking, and washing is a simple matter of turning on a faucet in the home; for the poor of Africa, it may require a daily trek of several miles.

Recognizing the importance of safe water, the United Nations established the target of halving the number of people who are without potable water and basic sanitation by the year 2015. This will entail bringing clean water to 1.5 billion individuals in developing countries and providing adequate sanitation facilities to another 2.1 billion.

In Africa many programs have incorporated low-cost technologies to bring safe water and sanitation to rural villages. Government workers and volunteers from NGOs and other charitable organizations have worked with villagers to improve water distribution systems. Programs have provided supplies and training for the installation of standpipes and pumps, and the digging of wells and boreholes to access clean water deep below the earth's surface. Other initiatives have focused on providing toilets or pit latrines in rural areas and constructing inexpensive sewerage systems in urban regions.

5 INSECT-BORNE DISEASES

While malaria is the deadliest vector-borne disease in Africa, many other similarly transmitted diseases afflict the continent's people. Insects serve as vectors for viruses (dengue fever, yellow fever, Rift Valley fever), parasites (African trypanosomiasis, leishmaniasis, onchocerciasis, filariasis), and bacteria (plague, relapsing fever). Although the majority of these diseases occur in rural areas, some spread quickly in overcrowded urban areas or refugee camps.

DENGUE FEVER AND DENGUE HEMORRHAGIC FEVER

(Opposite) The *Aedes aegypti* mosquito, which spreads viral diseases such as dengue fever, has expanded its range in tropical Africa. This insect's gut is red from the blood of the person upon whom it is feeding.

Dengue is caused by one of four viruses that are carried by the *Aedes aegypti* and *Aedes albopictus* mosquitoes. Dengue viruses are arboviruses, which means they are viruses carried by arthropods (such as mosquitoes and ticks). Dengue is the most widespread of arthropod-borne viruses and is endemic in the Middle East, the Far East,

and the Caribbean islands, as well as Africa. Each of the four dengue viruses causes disease, and exposure to one strain does not give immunity to another.

Symptoms of dengue usually occur about five to eight days after the victim has been bitten by an infected mosquito. Infants and young children typically suffer mild cases of dengue, characterized by a fever. Moderate cases of the disease, which occur more frequently in older children and adults, result in high fever, headaches, eye pain, enlarged lymph nodes, weakness, fatigue, and muscle and joint pain.

After two to three days of symptoms, the fever drops rapidly for about a day, then increases again. At this point, a rash of small red bumps appears on the arms, legs, and torso. When there are no complications, almost all patients recover from dengue fever. Infection can recur, however, although the body's immune system provides antibodies for about a year.

Severe cases of dengue fever, or dengue hemorrhagic fever (DHF), often occur in children who have had a previous dengue infection. Upon reinfection, the immune system overreacts, causing serious symptoms such as a very high fever, damage to the blood and lymph vessels, and bleeding from the nose, gums, and under the skin. DHF may lead to dengue shock syndrome, caused by the decrease of oxygen in the blood. Both of these complications of dengue can be fatal.

Blood tests can definitively diagnose infection by one of the four dengue viruses. Although there is no treatment to shorten the course of the disease, health workers may give medications to alleviate fever and body aches, as well as intravenous fluids to treat dehydration.

The World Health Organization estimates that there are 50 million to 100 million cases of dengue fever worldwide each year. While dengue fever rarely causes death, 2.5 percent to 5 percent of DHF cases are fatal, according to WHO estimates. Some 500,000 victims of DHF require hospitalization each year.

In Africa the number of cases of dengue fever has increased dramatically since the 1980s, particularly in eastern regions. Major epidemics have occurred in Kenya, Mozambique, Djibouti, and Somalia. No epidemics of DHF have occurred in Africa, although there are reports of individual cases.

As the *Aedes aegypti* mosquito has expanded its range in tropical areas of Africa, the dengue virus has spread as well. The disease can be found in urban as well as rural areas of the continent.

AFRICAN TRYPANOSOMIASIS (SLEEPING SICKNESS)

Found only in Africa, sleeping sickness (also called African trypanosomiasis) is caused by a single-celled protozoan parasite called *Trypanosoma*. It is spread by the tsetse fly, which lives along Africa's shores and riverbanks. When the fly bites a previously infected animal or human, it becomes infected. It then passes along the *Trypanosoma* protozoan when it bites again. In some parts of Africa where the tsetse fly is endemic, humans and animals cannot survive because of the disease carried by this deadly parasite.

The type of *Trypanosoma* protozoan that causes sleeping sickness in humans is the *Trypanosoma brucei* complex, which includes the subspecies *T. b. rhodesiense* (of southern and eastern Africa) and *T. b. gambiense* (of central and western Africa).

Because of the poor state of medical and health care infrastructure throughout the continent of Africa, the number of victims of sleeping sickness is impossible to know with any precision. While only about 40,000 to 45,000 new cases are reported each year, the World Health Organization estimates that up to 500,000 Africans contract the disease annually, with as many as 300,000 fatalities.

Two to three days after being bitten by an infected tsetse fly, the victim may see a sore at the site of the bite, soon followed by redness, pain, and swelling. As the parasite reproduces within the blood and lymphatic systems, symptoms of recurrent fever, headache, joint pain, and intense itching occur. Later, because the body's immune system is fighting the disease, symptoms may include swollen lymph nodes, enlarged liver and spleen, damaged organs, and leaking blood vessels.

If not treated during the first stage of the disease, sleeping sickness progresses to a second stage, in which the parasite attacks the central nervous system. Symptoms of the resulting neurological damage may include slurred speech, sensory disturbances, confusion, poor coordination, and deep sleep. If left untreated in this second stage, or if treatment is given too late, African trypanosomiasis eventually progresses (after several months or even years) to coma and death.

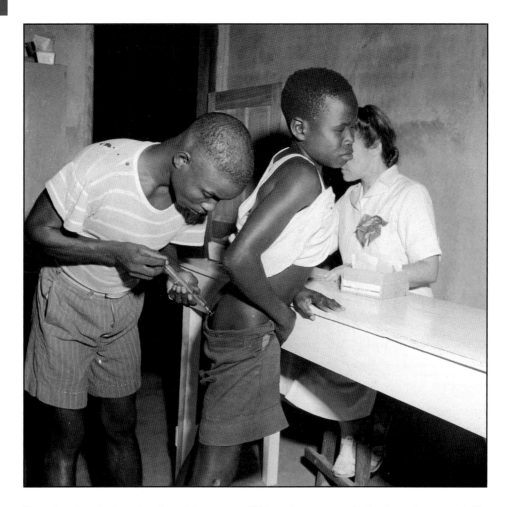

Drug treatments for sleeping sickness, or African trypanosomiasis, have been available for many decades; this photo, which shows a young patient receiving an injection for the disease, was taken around 1948, at a clinic in Liberia. But sleeping sickness continues to kill an estimated 300,000 Africans each year.

Physicians commonly treat sleeping sickness with toxic medications such as suramin, eflornithine, pentamidine, and several drugs that contain arsenic. These painful therapies have the potential to cause fatal allergic reactions, as well as kidney damage or inflammation of the brain. Other side effects to these drugs include diarrhea, abdominal pain, fever, and numbness.

Drug resistance is a growing problem with many of the medications used to treat African sleeping sickness. There are no vaccines to prevent the disease.

LEISHMANIASIS

A protozoan parasitic infection spread by the bite of tiny sand flies, leishmaniasis is found primarily in Asia, South America, and Africa. There are several types of leishmaniasis. Mucocutaneous leishmaniasis causes lesions in the nose, mouth, and throat. Cutaneous leishmaniasis causes skin sores and scarring all over the body. However, the most severe form of the disease is visceral leishmaniasis, also referred to as kala-azar, black fever, or sandfly disease. Symptoms include fever, weight loss, anemia, and swelling of the spleen and liver. If not treated, the disease is fatal. Visceral leishmaniasis affects 500,000 people each year, killing at least 200,000 annually. In Africa the disease strikes primarily in eastern and southern Sudan, mostly in the poorest rural areas of the country. During the 1990s, visceral leishmaniasis killed 100,000 people in Sudan.

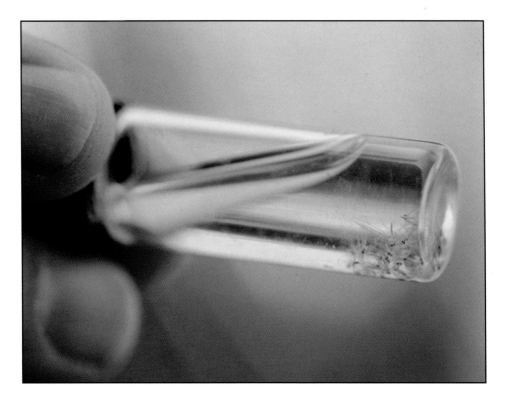

Tiny sand flies such as the ones in this vial are responsible for spreading leishmaniasis.

For more than 50 years, the usual treatments for leishmaniasis were antibiotics based on the chemical element antimony, or antimonials, injected daily over the course of 28 days. However, during a visceral leishmaniasis epidemic in southern Sudan in the early 1990s, doctors encountered drug resistance to the standard antimonial treatments. By combining antimony-based drugs with paromomycin, an inexpensive antibiotic previously used against intestinal parasites, health workers achieved better results.

Doctors have also used an antifungal medicine called amphotericin B, or fungizsone, to treat visceral leishmaniasis. Another drug recently found effective against the disease is miltefosine, but like antimony-based drugs, it is expensive. There is no effective vaccine for any form of leishmaniasis.

YELLOW FEVER

An estimated 200,000 cases of yellow fever occur each year, causing 20,000 to 30,000 deaths. The disease occurs only in Africa and South America, mostly in regions along the equator. The arbovirus that causes yellow fever is carried by the *Aedes aegypti* mosquito, the same vector that carries dengue fever. Within a few days of biting an infected person or animal, the mosquito becomes a carrier, capable of transmitting yellow fever with the next bite.

Symptoms of yellow fever appear three to six days after a person has been bitten by an infected mosquito. They include fever, chills, headache, dizziness, muscle pain, nausea, and vomiting. Patients usually suffer from these symptoms for about three or four days and then begin to recover.

However, in about 15 percent of yellow fever cases, the fever returns a few hours or days later, with serious consequences. A very high fever accompanies the deterioration of body organs, particularly the kidneys, liver, and heart. Damage to the liver causes jaundice. This condition results in the formation of yellow bile pigments in the skin, which turns the distinctive yellow color for which the disease is named.

Severe yellow fever soon progresses to a hemorrhagic illness, and the patient bleeds from the mouth, nose, eyes, and stomach. Once the disease reaches this stage, yellow fever kills about 5 percent of patients, who lapse into a coma and die within two weeks. Survivors of the disease acquire a lifelong immunity to the virus.

There are no antiviral treatments for yellow fever, and therapy consists of treating the symptoms with fever and pain relievers. Medication solutions may be given as well to replenish fluids lost to fever and bleeding.

A safe and effective vaccine to prevent infection with yellow fever was developed in 1937 by a South African research physician named Max Theiler. However, vaccinations of at-risk populations in Africa dropped after 1980, and since then the number of yellow fever cases has been on the rise. In 1992 epidemics of the disease occurred in Kenya and Liberia.

PLAGUE

Transmitted to humans by the bite of infected fleas living on rats, bubonic plague once killed hundreds of millions of people during epidemics in Europe and Asia. Records of plague date back to the 6th century A.D., when the disease wiped out up to 100 million people in the Mediterranean region. During the 14th century, an immense plague epidemic, referred to as the Black Death, killed one-third of Europe's population.

Today the plague is endemic in Africa: in 2003 Africa accounted for 98.9 percent of 182 deaths and 98.7 percent of the 2,118 reported cases worldwide. That year plague cases occurred in Angola, Botswana, the Democratic Republic of the Congo, Kenya, Madagascar, Malawi, Mozambique, Namibia, South Africa, Tanzania, Uganda, Zambia, and Zimbabwe.

Plague is caused by the bacterium *Yersinia pestis* (named for the French scientist Alexandre Yersin, who identified it in 1894). It is usually transmitted to humans by the bite of an infected flea. In bubonic plague, the *Yersinia pestis* bacteria attack the body's lymph nodes, causing painful swellings called buboes, usually located near the fleabites. If the bacteria enter the bloodstream and spread to other parts of the body, it is called septicemic plague. These same bacteria can also cause pneumonic plague, a bacterial infection in the lungs that can be transmitted in the air when an infected individual sneezes or coughs.

Symptoms of plague develop from one to eight days after the victim is infected and include high fever, headache, body ache, rapid heartbeat, and malaise. The disease is highly treatable if antibiotics are given soon after infection. If not treated, however, most plague victims die within five days.

ONCHOCERCIASIS (RIVER BLINDNESS)

Onchocerca volvulus, a tiny parasitic worm (filaria) transmitted by the bite of black flies, causes an eye and skin disease called onchocerciasis. The disease is also referred to as river blindness because it mostly affects people living near rapidly flowing rivers and streams, which serve as breeding grounds for the black flies that carry the tiny parasitic worms.

The vast majority of cases of river blindness occur in sub-Saharan Africa. There, approximately 18 million people have been infected with the parasite, with 6.5 million suffering from skin disease, or dermatitis, and about 270,000 suffering from blindness. Onchocerciasis is the world's second-leading cause of blindness, and it is most prevalent in Nigeria.

Onchocerca volvulus can live in the human body for a year, but it is actually the worm's larvae (microfilariae), which migrate to the skin and eyes, that cause the symptoms of onchocerciasis.

When the microfilariae die, they produce toxins that cause intense itching and damage to the skin, as well as the formation of lesions and scarring in the eye.

In 1974 the World Health Organization, the World Bank, Merck Pharmaceutical Company, the Food and Agriculture Organization, and the United Nations Development Program joined forces to defeat the disease through the efforts of the Onchocerciasis Control Program (OCP). To reduce the transmission of African river blindness, OCP sponsored aerial spraying of insecticides to lower or eradicate black fly populations. Starting in the late 1980s, OCP also began providing ivermectin (a drug used in veterinary medicine and donated by Merck) as a safe and effective treatment for eliminating onchocerciasis.

The boy shown in this photo lost his vision to onchocerciasis, which is also called river blindness. He and the two women are members of southern Sudan's Dinka people.

These efforts, OCP estimates, have prevented 600,000 cases of river blindness, made nearly 62 million acres (25 million hectares) safe for settlement and cultivation, and protected 40 million people.

RELAPSING FEVER

Relapsing fever gets its name from the cyclical nature of the disease. Victims suffer a high fever, chills, headache, and muscle ache, with symptoms lasting from several days to a week. This is followed by a period of seemingly good health, but then the symptoms return. The cycle can continue for as many as 10 episodes.

Relapsing fever (also sometimes called tick, recurrent, or famine fever) is caused by the bacterium *Borrelia spirochetes*, which is carried by lice or ticks. It is often found in areas with poor hygiene. Treatment includes elimination of the disease vector with delousing powder, as well as treatment with antibiotics such as erythromycin.

LYMPHATIC FILARIASIS

Transmitted by the *Anopheles* mosquito, lymphatic filariasis is an infection of the human lymphatic system by tiny, thread-like worms. More than 120 million people around the world have been affected by this disease, and over 40 million suffer serious disabilities and disfigurement because of it. One-third of those infected live in Africa.

The filariae responsible for lymphatic filariasis in Africa are called *Wuchereria bancrofti*. The tiny worms live and reproduce in the lymphatic system, where they cause swelling of the limbs and lymph nodes, which in severe cases develops into elephantiasis. This condition of massively enlarged limbs results from the blockage of the flow of lymph fluid to the limb, which causes it to swell up to several times its normal size. In African communities where lymphatic filariasis is endemic, 10 to 50 percent of men and up to 10 percent of women are affected. The disease also causes internal damage to the kidneys and lymphatic system.

The parasitic worms that cause this disease can live in the human body for four to six years. During that time they produce millions of larvae (microfilariae) that circulate in the blood; the adult worms, meanwhile, remain in the lymphatic system. Many people carry the filariae in their bodies without any apparent symptoms, although medical examinations will reveal lymphatic and kidney damage. Diagnosis of the disease is confirmed by microscopic examination of the blood for larval parasites.

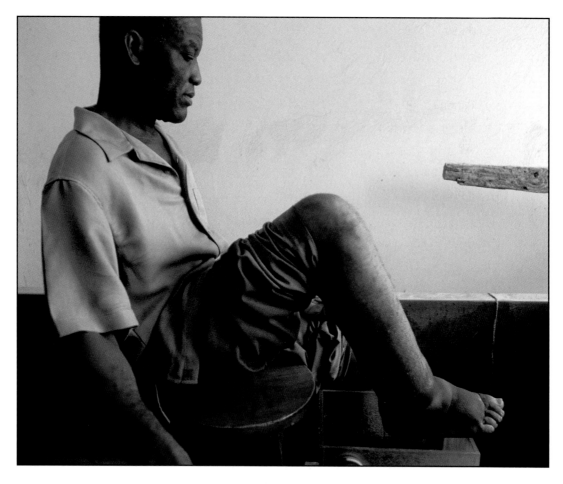

Lymphatic filariasis causes enlarged, disfigured limbs as well as damage to the kidneys and lymphatic system.

Recent studies have shown that the drug diethylcarba-mazine (DEC), previously given as 12-day doses, can be administered as a single dose and still provide up to a year's resistance to filariasis. The most effective treatment for removing the microfilariae from the blood appears to be the drug albendazole combined with either DEC or ivermectin (which is used in areas where onchocerciasis is endemic).

Donations by the pharmaceutical companies GlaxoSmith-Kline, which makes albendazole, and by Merck, which makes ivermectin, have allowed the World Health Organization to expand programs to eliminate the disease in Africa. These drugs have been given as mass treatments to at-risk populations to help reduce transmission from mosquito bites. The medications also improve elephantiasis when the disease is in the early stages. However, doses must be given yearly for four to six years. Cleansing and good hygiene of the affected limbs also helps reduce the severity of the condition.

RIFT VALLEY FEVER

A viral disease carried by mosquitoes, Rift Valley fever usually attacks livestock (cattle, sheep, goats, and camels), but it can also affect humans. Because it is a mosquito-borne disease, Rift Valley fever becomes prevalent after periods of unusually heavy rainfall and localized flooding. These conditions provide optimal breeding grounds for the mosquitoes (usually of the genus *Aedes*) that carry the Rift Valley fever virus.

First identified in Kenyan livestock during the early 1900s, Rift Valley fever is caused by a virus in the genus *Phlebovirus*. The disease is found mainly in eastern and southern Africa, although it affects most countries of sub-Saharan Africa to some degree. An epidemic in animals has been known to lead to epidemics in humans. One of the most serious outbreaks of Rift Valley fever occurred in Egypt in 1977, at which time several million people were infected and thousands died. Another significant epidemic occurred in 1987, in West Africa.

Humans get Rift Valley fever from infected mosquitoes, although they may also contract the disease from contact with the blood or body fluids of infected animals. People most at risk of contracting Rift Valley fever work with animals as herders, veterinarians, or slaughterhouse employees in areas where the virus is present.

Symptoms of the disease can be nonexistent or mild, consisting of fever, weakness, back pain, dizziness, and weight loss. Recovery takes two days to a week. However, Rift Valley fever can also progress to hemorrhagic fever, encephalitis (inflammation or swelling of the brain), or diseases affecting the eye that can cause blindness. Death occurs in about 1 percent of the cases of Rift Valley fever infection. Although there is no standard course of treatment for victims of the virus, the antiviral drug ribavirin can shorten the duration of the disease.

PREVENTING THE SPREAD OF INSECT-BORNE DISEASE

Education can play a major role in preventing the spread of insect-borne disease. If people know what is causing them to become ill, they can take the necessary measures to prevent infection—such as using insect repellents and pesticide-treated bed nets. Bed netting can also be used with sick patients to prevent mosquitoes from biting them and continuing the disease transmission cycle.

Another important way to prevent insect-borne diseases such as malaria, dengue, and yellow fever is to reduce or eradicate the insect populations responsible for spreading the pathogens (the bacteria or viruses that cause the diseases). This is accomplished by spraying insecticides in homes, eliminating sources of standing water (where disease-carrying mosquitoes can breed), and

In addition to spreading malaria, mosquitoes transmit yellow fever, lymphatic filariasis, Rift Valley fever, and dengue fever. This roadside billboard urges Zambians to strike back at the insects by using insecticide-treated nets.

clearing animal waste (which attracts the sand flies that carry kala-azar parasites).

Technology can also help reduce insect populations. One way to prevent insects from reproducing is to sterilize the males with radiation or chemicals, and then release them within a specific area. Females that mate with the sterilized insects will produce eggs that do not yield offspring. This method of insect control, called sterile-insect technique (SIT), requires the continuing release of large numbers of sterilized males into the environment to keep the wild bug population low.

The SIT method is not feasible in the wide-open spaces of the African mainland. However, it has proved effective in contained areas such as the Tanzanian island of Zanzibar, where in the 1990s it eradicated the tsetse fly population.

A 2004 story in *Science News* reported that genetic engineering, rather than chemicals or radiation, can also be used to selectively reduce insect fertility. Some researchers are working to stop the spread of dengue fever and yellow fever by reducing the ability of the *Aedes aegypti* mosquito to reproduce. Through genetic engineering, the scientists hope to alter the insect's genes so that the male cannot produce females. Without females to spread disease and reproduce, this mosquito species would be eradicated.

Some scientists are using genetic engineering not to block insect reproduction, but rather to alter bugs' ability to transmit parasites, bacteria, or viruses. Researchers have developed a strain of the malaria-carrying *Anopheles* mosquito that does not allow malaria parasites to mature within its gut or spread to new hosts. Researchers at Yale University have modified bacteria found in the tsetse fly so they create chemicals that kill the parasite responsible for sleeping sickness. However, these genetically engineered species do not have the ability to survive and thrive in the wild.

The use of genetic engineering remains controversial. Some African countries have already banned genetically modified crops; insect control using genetic engineering could meet with the same opposition. However, the potential of this scientific field to help control or eradicate certain human diseases has attracted significant research funding. In 2003 a major contributor, the Bill & Melinda Gates Foundation, identified the development of "a genetic strategy to deplete or incapacitate a disease-transmitting insect population" as one of 14 "grand challenges in global health."

In July 2005, researchers announced that they had successfully mapped the genes of parasites that cause African sleeping sickness and visceral leishmaniasis. This research may make possible the development of drugs or vaccines to fight these trypanosome parasites, as well as further the development of diagnostic tests to identify and treat these illnesses.

6 VIRAL HEMORRHAGIC FEVERS

iral hemorrhagic fevers do not cause many deaths in Africa, especially when compared with the numbers killed by AIDS, tuberculosis, and malaria. However, when epidemics of viral hemorrhagic fever occur, the media pay close attention. The horrific symptoms of massive bleeding within the body, combined with the sudden onset and high death rates of these diseases, make them among the world's most feared.

The term *viral hemorrhagic fever* refers to any of a group of illnesses caused by viruses that attack blood vessels and multiple organs in the body, causing heavy bleeding, or hemorrhage. Among the most well known hemorrhagic fevers are Ebola, Marburg, and Lassa. These viruses spread from human to human—through contact with infected people or their body fluids. Contact with objects that have been contaminated with infected body fluids can also cause infection. In fact, contaminated medical supplies, such as syringes and needles, are believed to

(Opposite) A Red Cross worker disinfects a hospital room while a patient stricken with Ebola hemorrhagic fever lies on a bed, Republic of the Congo, March 2003. More than 125 people—including every adult in the remote village of Ndjoukou—died in the 2003 Ebola outbreak in the northwestern part of the Congo.

have caused past outbreaks of Ebola hemorrhagic fever and Lassa fever.

Some hemorrhagic fevers develop from treatable diseases such as dengue fever, yellow fever, and Rift Valley fever, which are spread by arthropod vectors, and not by person-to-person contact. Once these fevers develop into hemorrhagic forms, the chances for survival are greatly reduced. However, the mortality rates for these diseases are not as stark as those for Ebola or Marburg.

EBOLA

Perhaps the best-known viral hemorrhagic fever in Africa is Ebola. Named for the Ebola River in northern Congo, where the first human cases were identified, the disease attacks humans and other primates, usually with fatal results. Very few people survive Ebola, which has a mortality rate of 80 to 90 percent.

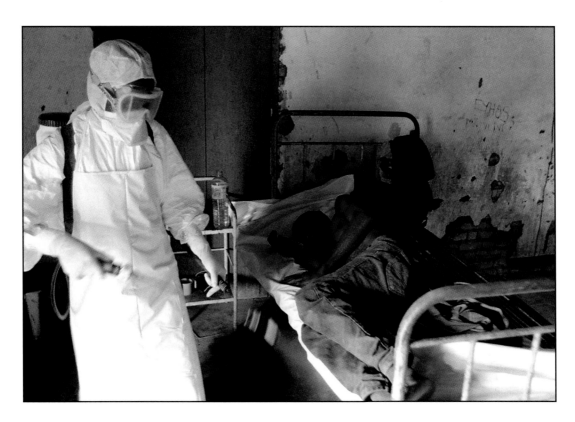

The first signs of Ebola appear similar to those of malaria or flu: sore throat, headache, and fever. Bouts of nausea, vomiting, and diarrhea soon follow. As the Ebola virus reproduces itself within the body, it spreads through the blood to the organs, targeting the liver, kidneys, spleen, and reproductive organs. Soon the major organs and smaller blood vessels begin to bleed. Massive internal bleeding ultimately causes kidney failure, shock, and respiratory problems that lead to death.

The Ebola virus is transmitted by contact with the bodily fluids—such as the mucus, saliva, sweat, and blood—of an infected person. It can also be passed on by contaminated needles or other medical equipment. Symptoms may appear anytime from a few days to two weeks after exposure.

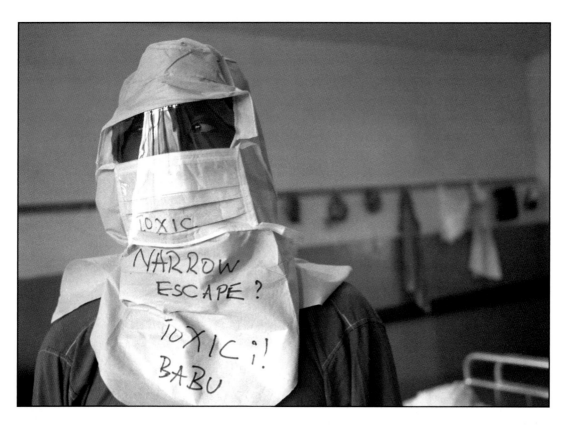

The Ugandan nurse shown here caught Ebola twice during an outbreak in 2000 and 2001. He beat the odds: the death rate for those with Ebola hemorrhagic fever ranges up to 90 percent, and hospital staff caring for patients are often among the victims.

During the mid-1970s, a series of disease outbreaks killed approximately 440 people in western Sudan and Zaire (now known as the Democratic Republic of the Congo). Almost 90 percent of those who contracted the disease died from it. Another major outbreak of the Ebola virus occurred in 1995, in and around the town of Kikwit, in the Congo. Only 50 of the 300 victims survived. Some researchers believe that a May 2005 outbreak in northwestern Congo occurred because villagers ate the body of an Ebola-infected chimpanzee. Smaller outbreaks of Ebola have occurred in Côte d'Ivoire, Gabon, and northern Uganda.

Epidemics of Ebola can kill hundreds of people at a time. There is no cure for the disease, so medical teams respond to outbreaks by educating people about how to avoid infection and by isolating Ebola victims.

MARBURG

Named for the town in Germany where the first recorded outbreak occurred, among workers at a research laboratory, Marburg fever is closely related to Ebola. The disease is believed to have originated in Uganda and eastern Congo, the source of infected African green monkeys that were being used in the Marburg lab. Of the 25 persons infected in Marburg and Frankfurt during the 1967 outbreak, 7 died.

A severe form of hemorrhagic fever, Marburg shares many of the same symptoms as Ebola: vomiting, bloody discharge, and fever, with death occurring between three and seven days after onset of symptoms. Diagnosis of the virus is confirmed by analysis of blood samples. Like Ebola, the mortality rate for Marburg fever is high.

Until 2005, the worst epidemic of Marburg had occurred in Congo between 1998 and 2000, at which time about 100 cases were recorded. However, in March 2005, health authorities in Angola learned of a massive outbreak involving hundreds of people living in Uige, a northern province of the country that borders

Congo. By April, 266 cases of Marburg had been recorded, and 244 of the victims had died. According to the World Health Organization, three-quarters of the victims were children. However, health officials also reported that the rate of new cases decreased as people began to understand how to prevent the disease from spreading. The outbreak was finally declared contained in September. By then, according to Angola's Ministry of Health, there had been 374 cases, with 329 deaths.

PREVENTING THE SPREAD OF EBOLA AND MARBURG

Because there is no cure for Ebola or Marburg, medical workers must take a two-pronged approach in dealing with epidemics. First, they need to educate communities about how the disease is spread in order to ensure that families of infected patients do not have direct contact with their body fluids—when alive or dead. In some African countries, such as Uganda, local funeral traditions involve washing the dead, a practice that can easily spread the disease. Second, medical staff must be vigilant about maintaining aseptic procedures in hospitals and clinics where Ebola or Marburg patients are being treated. Health workers must wear gloves, masks, and other protective clothing while treating patients, in order to avoid coming into contact with infected bodily fluids. Medical instruments and equipment must be properly sterilized. And patients with viral hemorrhagic fever need to be isolated from other patients (commonly accomplished through the use of sheets of plastic to separate isolation wards from other units). Unfortunately, such efforts to prevent the spread of hemorrhagic virus infections have often alienated patients' family members, who do not understand why they cannot have contact with their loved ones.

During the early stages of the 2005 Marburg outbreak in Angola, many families distrusted the medical teams that were working to keep the infected patients isolated. Rather than hospitalize stricken family members, some people hid them and, when they died, buried them secretly so they could be put to rest according to traditional rituals. Soon the survivors became ill themselves. The rate of disease transmission began to decrease only after people understood that the only way to prevent the spread of the disease was by isolating the infected people.

LASSA FEVER

Although related to Ebola and Marburg, Lassa fever is not as severe. It is, however, much more common: the number of annual cases of Lassa fever is many times higher than the number of Ebola and Marburg cases combined. Lassa disease is endemic in West Africa, especially in rural areas, where hundreds of thousands of people are infected each year.

About 80 percent of the people who are infected with the Lassa virus either develop mild symptoms or have no symptoms at all. The other 20 percent suffer from a severe form of the illness, and 2 percent of them die. In fact, Lassa fever claims several thousand victims in Africa every year. Among those most likely to die from Lassa fever are women in the late stages of pregnancy and the babies they are carrying. The most common complication of the disease is deafness.

First identified in the 1960s, when an epidemic broke out in Nigeria, Lassa fever is usually transmitted by rats. However, the infection can also be transmitted from an infected person to a healthy one. Some patients have been helped by treatment with ribavirin, an antiviral drug.

POSSIBLE FUTURE VACCINES

In June 2005, scientists from Canada, France, and the United States announced that they had taken steps toward creating a vaccine for Ebola and Marburg. To do so, they made genetic

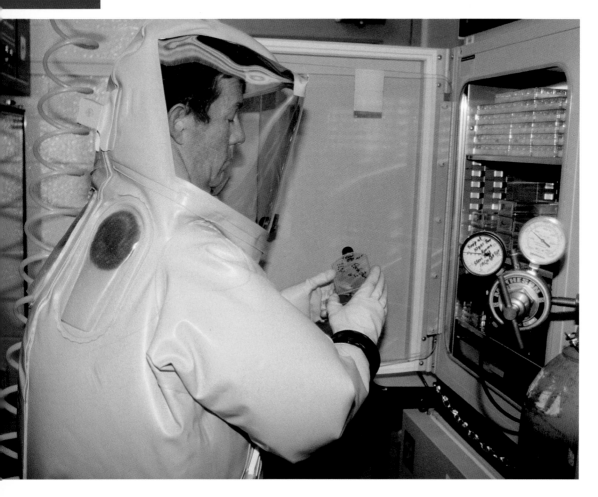

Protected by a biohazard suit, a scientist at the United States Medical Research Institute of Infectious Diseases, in Fort Detrick, Maryland, handles an Ebola sample. Work on vaccines against the Ebola, Marburg, and Lassa viruses is under way in various countries, including the United States, France, and Canada.

adaptations to a separate virus so that it could carry proteins from Ebola and Marburg. When this altered virus was injected into macaque monkeys that were subsequently exposed to Ebola or Marburg, the primates did not develop the hemorrhagic diseases. Other research using the antibodies from the marrow of Ebola survivors may play a part in developing treatments for victims of the disease.

Research has already produced a separate Ebola vaccine, which is based on the virus that causes the common cold in people. The vaccine protected monkeys in tests run in 2003 and was slated for human testing in 2005.

A vaccine against Lassa fever is also in the early stages of development. In June 2005, a team from the U.S. Army Medical Research Institute for Infectious Diseases and the Public Health Agency of Canada reported the successful vaccination of macaques against the Lassa virus. The vaccine contains protein from the Lassa virus that is carried by a harmless virus. When injected into the monkeys, the dose kept them from developing the disease.

7 VACCINE-PREVENTABLE DISEASES

Many diseases that have been conquered in industrialized nations continue to kill millions of people in developing nations, particularly in the poor countries of Africa. Worldwide, more than 2 million children in developing countries die each year from vaccine-preventable diseases. Many more become disabled by illnesses that do not occur in industrialized nations because of widespread immunizations.

MEASLES

Measles is a leading cause of death among children in Africa. According to the UNICEF website, the disease claims one African child every minute, mostly in regions where there is great poverty and inadequate health care. Of the approximately 12 million African children under age 15 who develop measles each year, some 450,000 to 500,000 die. The disease accounts for 56 percent of all vaccine-preventable deaths on the continent.

(Opposite) Widespread vaccination has virtually eliminated measles in the United States, but each year the disease continues to strike about 12 million Africans under age 15, claiming the lives of up to 500,000 of them. This Nigerian child is recovering from the disease.

A highly contagious disease, measles is caused by a type of virus called a paramyxovirus. The disease affects the respiratory system, skin, and eyes and is transmitted through the air when infected individuals sneeze or cough. People who have not been vaccinated against measles can contract the disease when they breathe in the droplets or come into contact with an infected surface (the virus can survive for up to two hours outside a host). Although measles symptoms do not occur until 7 to 18 days later, the newly infected person is most contagious 3 to 5 days before he or she actually becomes ill.

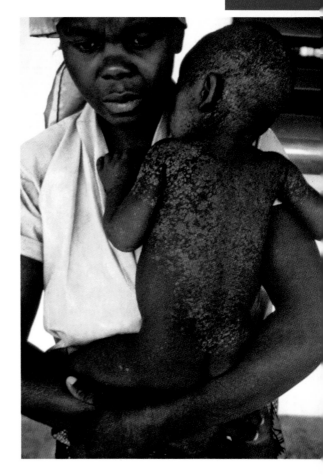

Initial symptoms of measles include a high fever, runny nose, and cough, followed a few days later by a characteristic rash (flat, red patches that develop into bumps). Complications from measles can include severe diarrhea, pneumonia, encephalitis, and secondary infections leading to deafness or blindness. In fact, measles is the leading cause of preventable blindness in the world, according to the World Health Organization.

Measles is easily diagnosed by its characteristic rash, which spreads out from the torso and covers the face, arms, and legs. There are no drugs to cure the disease, although medications are used to help relieve symptoms such as fever, and antibiotics may be given to prevent possible bacterial infection. Large doses of vitamin A may also be provided, since several studies have shown that these supplements can significantly reduce complication and death rates from measles. Once a person has had the measles, the body is immune from reinfection.

In 1963 an effective vaccine for measles became available in much of the developed world. It consists of live measles viruses that have been weakened so that they do not cause the disease. Although measles immunization is widespread in industrialized nations, children in Africa have had limited access. Even today, the majority of measles deaths occur in countries where immunization coverage for children is less than 50 percent.

HIB DISEASES

Almost one-fifth of vaccine-preventable childhood deaths occur from infections by *Haemophilus influenzae* type b (Hib) bacteria, which can cause bacterial pneumonia and bacterial meningitis. Hib infections kill an estimated 100,000 to 160,000 children in sub-Saharan Africa each year.

An infection of the lungs, pneumonia can be caused by viruses, bacteria, fungi, and other agents. However, bacterial pneumonia results mostly from infections by *Haemophilus influenzae*, *Streptococcus pneumoniae*, and *Staphylococcus aureus*.

Symptoms of pneumonia reflect the efforts of the body's immune system to fight the bacterial infection of the lung's alveoli. The air sacs become inflamed, and fever, cough, chest pain, and shortness of breath result. Pneumonia symptoms also include rapid respiration and coughing that brings up mucus streaked with pus or blood. Parts of the lung fill with fluid and the debris from dead white blood cells that battled the bacteria. Penicillin antibiotics can be quite effective in treating bacterial pneumonia, especially when administered soon after the first symptoms appear.

Meningitis, which is an inflammation of the meninges (the membrane layers covering the spinal cord and brain), can also be caused by bacteria, viruses, or fungi. However, bacterial meningitis is the deadliest form of this disease. The three bacteria responsible for the majority of bacterial meningitis cases are *Haemophilus influenzae* type b, *Neisseria meningitidis* (which causes meningococcal meningitis), and *Streptococcus pneumoniae* (which causes pneumococcal meningitis). Worldwide, bacterial meningitis accounts for at least 1.2 million cases and about 171,000 deaths per year.

The bacteria that cause meningitis live naturally in the back of the nose and throat without causing any symptoms. These bacteria are transmitted in the air when people cough or sneeze, and they can also be spread in saliva when people share cups and utensils without washing them. Meningitis develops when the bacteria in the nose, throat, and sinus cavities make their way into the bloodstream.

Symptoms of meningitis include fever, severe headache, nausea, vomiting, sensitivity to light, fatigue, a reddish purple rash, and a stiff neck. If not treated, the illness can progress rapidly and cause serious neurological damage, coma, and death. Brain damage from meningitis can cause lifelong problems, including epilepsy, learning disabilities, blindness, and hearing loss.

Physicians treat meningitis intravenously with antibiotics such as penicillin and cephalosporins. Because bacterial meningitis progresses rapidly— infection can lead to coma and death in as little as one day—victims of the disease need to be treated quickly.

In industrialized countries the vaccine to prevent Hib infection has been part of standard childhood

Widespread vaccination is a critical component of strategies to reduce Africa's high child mortality rates. Here infants are immunized in Ghana.

immunizations since the late 1980s. Increasing use of the vaccine in the developing world has significantly reduced the number of cases of *H. influenzae* type b meningitis there as well.

NEONATAL TETANUS

Although extremely rare in the industrial world, tetanus is the third-greatest vaccine-preventable killer of children in Africa, accounting for an estimated 15 percent of such deaths. The Centers for Disease Control and Prevention has estimated that more than 270,000 mothers and infants die from maternal and neonatal tetanus each year.

Tetanus is caused by the spores of a bacterium called *Clostridium tetani,* which occurs naturally in the soil and in animal waste. After entering the human body through a wound or cut, the spores germinate, producing a highly toxic poison. In neonatal (or infant) tetanus, the bacteria enter into the mother's and baby's bloodstream at birth when dirty tools are used to cut the umbilical cord or when incisions are covered with contaminated bandages.

Once inside the body, the tetanus bacteria attack the nervous system. After 2 to 50 days, symptoms such as convulsive spasms and tightened muscles occur. Another name for tetanus is "lockjaw," which describes the common symptom of tetanus that leads to death—the inability to open the mouth or swallow. Tetanus may eventually lead to respiratory paralysis, a condition in which the patient is unable to breathe. Neonatal tetanus has a mortality rate of more than 90 percent.

The majority of mothers and newborns killed by tetanus live in areas of extreme poverty, where they have had little access to information on safe childbirth practices. The disease is especially severe in the Democratic Republic of the Congo, Ethiopia, Nigeria, and Somalia.

Tetanus can be prevented through immunization and through hygienic child delivery practices. The Initiative to Eliminate Maternal and Neonatal Tetanus works to help fund and deliver vaccines to countries where the disease is still a major public health problem. Immunization efforts have practically eliminated neonatal tetanus in many developing countries, most recently in the African nations of Malawi, Namibia, South Africa, and Zimbabwe.

The World Health Organization recommends that three doses of the vaccine tetanus toxoid (TT) be given to all women of child-bearing age in high-risk areas. Protection lasts for 15 years; it can be passed along to newborns for the first few months of life.

WHOOPING COUGH

About 30 million to 50 million cases of whooping cough, or pertussis, occur around the world each year, mostly in developing countries. The disease annually kills about 300,000. In Africa, pertussis is the cause of an estimated 12 percent of all vaccine-preventable childhood deaths.

Whooping cough is caused by a bacterium, *Bordetella pertussis*, which infects the lungs. This highly contagious disease spreads through infected droplets in the air that have been discharged by the coughing or sneezing of an infected person. Once inhaled into the lungs, the bacteria multiply within the tissues of the respiratory tract.

About 7 to 14 days after infection, the first symptoms appear: coughing, sneezing, and a runny nose. One to two weeks later, the cough becomes much worse: the patient is wracked by uncontrollable spasms or fits of coughing that are followed by a sharp intake of breath, producing the rasping, or "whooping," sound that gives the disease its name. These coughing fits will either slack off over the course of one or two months and the patient will improve, or futher complications—

such as pneumonia, encephalitis, or secondary bacterial infection—will follow.

Treatment with the antibiotic erythromycin can slow the spread of *B. pertussis* during the early stages of whooping cough and make the patient less infectious. However, no treatment can stop the progression of the disease. Additional care can include provision of fluids to prevent dehydration. The vaccine against pertussis, given in combination with vaccines for the diseases of diphtheria and tetanus, is called the DPT vaccine.

DIPHTHERIA

Endemic in Egypt, Algeria, and many countries in sub-Saharan Africa, diphtheria is an acute bacterial infection caused by *Corynebacterium diphtheriae*. The bacteria, which attack the nose, throat, tonsils, and/or skin, release toxins that enter the lymph system and bloodstream. The disease causes breakdown of tissues of many parts of the body, including the heart, muscle, nerves, kidneys, liver, and spleen.

Diphtheria usually affects children ages 15 and younger. It is easily spread when the infected person coughs or sneezes, or by physical contact with discharge from the nose, throat, eyes, or skin lesions. Outbreaks of diphtheria commonly occur where people live together in crowded conditions.

Symptoms of diphtheria usually develop two to four days after infection. They include a sore throat, low-grade fever, and enlarged lymph nodes in the neck. If the skin is infected, painful skin lesions develop and become reddened and swollen.

The disease can be cured with the use of antibiotics such as penicillin and erythromycin. If it is not treated, however, complications such as breathing problems, heart failure, paralysis, and blood disorders may occur, and in 5 to 10 percent of cases, the patient will die. The DPT vaccine, administered to infants and children, is effective in preventing diphtheria.

POLIOMYELITIS (POLIO)

A highly contagious viral infection of the nervous system, poliomyelitis (polio) can cause paralysis or death within just a few hours of infection. This disease is spread by contact with infected individuals, through water or food that has been contaminated with human waste, or from infected droplets discharged by the sneezing or coughing of an infected person. Once in the body, the virus is absorbed into the bloodstream and lymphatic system, where it continues to multiply until reaching the brain and spinal cord. Polio strikes primarily where sanitation is poor and children are malnourished.

In the majority of cases, polio occurs in a minor form. Symptoms, which appear 3 to 21 days after infection, include a slight fever, fatigue, headache, sore throat, and vomiting. Young children account for most illnesses in this mild form, and recovery from the disease usually follows within 24 to 72 hours. Older children and adults are more likely to be struck by the major illness (about 10 percent of infections), which causes severe headache, and pain and stiffness in the lower back and neck. These symptoms occur because the virus causes inflammation of the meninges, or viral meningitis. Recovery can take several days.

In approximately 1 percent of polio cases, the disease inflames and attacks the body's motor nerves, causing paralysis of certain muscles. Paralysis from polio infection is not always permanent. When the nerve cells have not been completely destroyed, recovery may be possible within one to six months if the body can replace the lost nerves. If all nerve cells have been lost, paralysis is permanent.

In about half of the cases of major illness, patients will completely recover; about one-quarter of the patients will be left with a slight disability, and one-quarter will have a permanent, serious disability. In about 1 percent of major polio cases, death comes

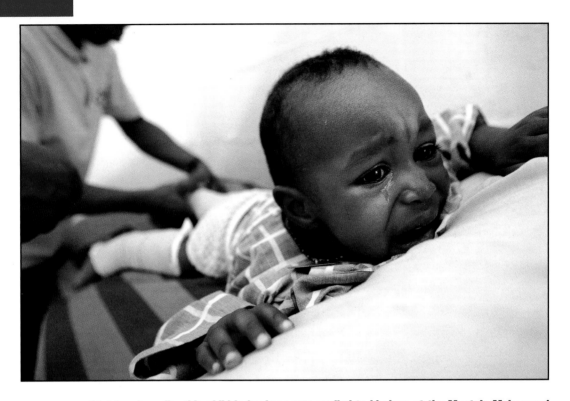

Stricken by polio, this child is having casts applied to his legs at the Murtala Muhammed Public Hospital in Kano, Nigeria, April 2005. In the wake of the U.S.-led "war on terrorism," Muslim clerics in the Nigerian state of Kano admonished followers not to have their children vaccinated against polio, saying that the United States was using the vaccine to sterilize the children. An outbreak of polio soon followed in northern Nigeria, and by 2003 the disease had spread to the West African nations of Burkina Faso, Ghana, Niger, and Togo.

quickly as the virus invades the parts of the brain that control breathing and swallowing, heart rate, and blood pressure.

In 1950 polio killed half a million people and was the fifth-leading cause of death and disability in children around the world. Five years later, the first effective vaccine against the disease was introduced by Jonas Salk. Given by a series of injections, it consisted of killed poliovirus. An oral polio vaccine consisting of live, weakened poliovirus was later developed by Albert Bruce Sabin. Both vaccines proved effective in providing immunity against the poliovirus, and the disease soon became rare in the industrialized world. However, large-scale immunization efforts did not begin in Africa until 1988, through the Global Polio Eradication Initiative.

MENINGOCOCCAL DISEASE

Caused by the *Neisseria meningitidis* bacterium, meningococcal disease is the only form of bacterial meningitis that can cause epidemics. It is spread through respiratory droplets produced by coughing or sneezing. Although there are many strains of meningococcus, the type A strain is found predominantly in sub-Saharan Africa.

N. meningitidis epidemics have caused thousands of deaths, mostly in West and Central African countries. In fact, the area extending from Senegal to Ethiopia has been referred to as the "meningitis belt" because of the high number of cases of the disease that occur there. Meningitis epidemics tend to occur in irregular cycles every 5 to 12 years, and death rates can be high. In 1996 an epidemic in sub-Saharan Africa resulted in approximately 200,000 cases and 20,000 deaths. About 75 percent of cases occur in children less than 15 years old.

If not treated, meningococcal meningitis can cause death in 80 percent of those afflicted. Treatment lowers the death rate dramatically, to between 5 percent and 15 percent. Humanitarian organizations have found that mass vaccination with the meningococcal type A&C vaccine is the best way to prevent the spread of the disease.

PNEUMOCOCCUS DISEASES

The bacterium *Streptococcus pneumoniae*, or pneumococcus, is responsible for most cases of pneumonia. *S. pneumoniae* also causes infections in the bloodstream (bacteremia, or blood sepsis) and in the tissue and fluids around the brain and spinal cord (meningitis). The World Health Organization estimates that 700,000 to 1 million children in developing countries die each year because of pneumococcal pneumonia and pneumococcal meningitis. A vaccine against *S. pneumoniae* is under development and has been

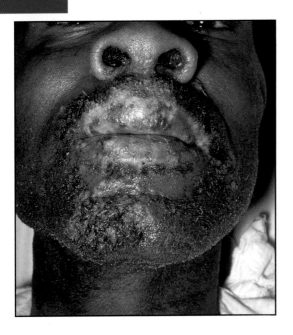

Lesions on the face of a pneumococcal meningitis patient in Africa. Pneumococcal meningitis can be treated with intravenous antibiotics, but the disease progresses very rapidly.

tested with some success in the West African country of Gambia.

OBSTACLES TO VACCINATION

Many barriers have stood in the way of the widespread immunization of Africa's children. For the continent's many impoverished nations, the cost of vaccinations can be a major hurdle. In addition, health care infrastructure tends to be weak or nonexistent in urban slums and in remote villages, where many children live. Immunization programs also face major obstacles in bringing vaccines to the children of nomadic families, which move from region to region with their herds, or to children who have been displaced by wars and civil unrest. Logistical difficulties often are compounded by cultural barriers: because of their religious or traditional beliefs, some African parents are suspicious of immunization.

In efforts to provide vaccinations to Africa's children, humanitarian groups send mobile teams to remote villages and meeting places, where they work with community leaders and religious leaders to educate them about the lifesaving importance of immunization. Once cooperation is established, health workers establish schedules that allow them to administer vaccines to entire populations on one day or over the course of several days (known as national immunization days, or NIDs), rather than trying to deliver vaccines to remote areas throughout the year.

During NIDs, health workers and volunteers administer vaccines against polio or measles and distribute vitamin A capsules. Vaccinations take place not only at hospitals and health clinics, but also at local government offices, schools, churches, mosques, and marketplaces.

Even warfare has not stopped immunization programs. In order to allow immunization teams to safely reach regions where children are at high risk of disease, UNICEF and other UN organizations have negotiated temporary cease-fires between warring factions. In 2001, despite ongoing conflict in the Democratic Republic of the Congo, health workers immunized more than 11 million children on NIDs.

Vaccination efforts take on even greater urgency in refugee camps, which are typically crowded with the survivors of disasters such as drought, famine, or warfare. Many vaccine-preventable illnesses—including yellow fever, measles, and meningitis—spread quickly among malnourished and weakened people, especially those living in places where sanitation is inadequate.

EXPANDED PROGRAM ON IMMUNIZATION (EPI)

In 1974 the World Health Organization launched an effort to increase the number of vaccinations given to children in poor countries. At that time, fewer than 5 percent of children in developing countries were immunized against the top killers: polio, diphtheria, tuberculosis, whooping cough, measles, and tetanus. Called the Expanded Program on Immunization (EPI), the program has been quite effective in reaching millions of at-risk children. Worldwide, nearly 75 percent of children have received vaccinations because of EPI. However, that record is far lower in sub-Saharan Africa, where the rate of immunization coverage had fallen below 50 percent by 2000. In the poorest countries of Africa, that percentage was below 35 percent.

MEASLES INITIATIVE

In February 2001, representatives of the American Red Cross, the U.S. Centers for Disease Control and Prevention, UNICEF, the United Nations Foundation, and the World Health Organization met to discuss disease in Africa. They eventually set a goal, in partnership with the International Federation of Red Cross and Red Crescent Societies and the governments of many African nations, to vaccinate 200 million children in Africa against measles by the year 2006.

By 2003 more than 100 million children in 25 African countries had been vaccinated. As a result of the initiative, the number of measles cases in Africa decreased by 46 percent between 1999 and 2003. As of 2004 a total of 36 sub-Saharan African countries had participated in mass vaccinations against measles, at a cost of approximately $200 million.

THE GLOBAL POLIO ERADICATION INITIATIVE

In 1988 the World Health Organization established the Global Polio Eradication Initiative, a program to bring about worldwide immunizations against polio. At that time polio was endemic in more than 125 countries. Numerous organizations, including UNICEF, Rotary International, the International Red Cross and Red Crescent Societies, and the U.S. Centers for Disease Control and Prevention, as well as governments and volunteer groups, set up mass immunization campaigns to administer polio vaccines to children in these countries. Financial support came from private sector foundations, as well as from development banks, donor countries, and corporate partners such as Sanofi Pasteur, De Beers, and Wyeth Pharmaceuticals.

The typical effort to bring polio vaccine to Africans during national immunization days is described on the UNICEF website:

National immunization days are designed to bring vaccinations to entire sections of the population, particularly in rural or remote areas, during a single focused campaign. Here Red Cross workers go door-to-door in a Kenyan village as part of a national immunization day.

> During each NID (normally three or four days long), tens of thousands of vaccinators fan out to every corner of a polio endemic-country, carrying the polio vaccine in a plastic or styrofoam "cold box" on their shoulders. Their mission is to reach every child under five and immunize them at their doorsteps.

The oral polio vaccine is administered in two doses at NIDs held one month apart. No matter how remote the location, health workers must haul iceboxes and refrigerator units, as the vaccine needs to remain cold to be effective.

From 1990 through 2005, thanks to the efforts of the Global Polio Eradication Initiative, more than 10 billion doses of oral polio vaccine were delivered to over 2 billion children throughout the world. Approximately 20 million volunteers and $3 billion in funding helped the initiative decrease the number of polio cases worldwide by more than 99 percent—from 350,000 in 1988 to just 784 in 2003. At that time, the disease was endemic in only six countries—three in Asia (India, Pakistan, and Afghanistan) and three in Africa (Nigeria, Niger, and Egypt).

Unfortunately, that year Nigeria halted its immunization campaign because of civil unrest and local suspicions about the polio vaccine. Some feared it was contaminated with AIDS; others believed it would make their children sterile. As a result, the number of children with polio in Nigeria alone rose to 788 in 2004.

Immunization rates also dropped in several other African countries, including Côte d'Ivoire, Burkina Faso, the Central African Republic, Sudan, and Ethiopia. By 2004 outbreaks of polio were reported in 12 African countries that previously had been free of the disease.

In mid-2004 immunization efforts resumed in Nigeria, but at the end of that year, the country accounted for two-thirds of the world's new polio cases. Vaccination efforts continued, however, and in December 2004 the Global Polio Eradication Initiative reported the successful immunization of 80 million children through synchronized polio campaigns across 23 countries in Africa.

Plans to continue reaching at-risk children in Nigeria and other African countries require ongoing funding. Expenses for 2006 alone have been estimated at $200 million.

GLOBAL ALLIANCE FOR VACCINES AND IMMUNIZATION

Launched in 2000 to guide and coordinate child-immunization efforts, the Global Alliance for Vaccines and Immunization (GAVI) brings together a variety of public- and private-sector entities, including the governments of industrialized and developing countries, vaccine manufacturers, UN agencies, and charitable foundations. Much of GAVI's initial funding came in 1999 from the Bill & Melinda Gates Foundation, which donated $750 million for use over a five-year period.

Administering an oral polio vaccine, South Africa. A variety of initiatives sponsored by the United Nations, international aid agencies, and charitable organizations are attempting to bring the benefits of vaccination to Africa's people, but much work remains.

Numerous national governments have also lent financial support.

In January 2005 the Gates Foundation followed up on its initial gift with another $750 million donation, which is intended for use over the next 10 years. During that period GAVI aims to give vaccine protection to 90 percent of newborn children in the regions where it is working. In 2004 the organization reported that 41.6 million children had been vaccinated against hepatitis B and 5.6 million against *Haemophilus influenzae* type b (Hib); an additional 3.2 million had received the vaccine against yellow fever, and 9.6 million had been given other basic vaccines.

GAVI also provides support to encourage private industry in vaccine development and research.

GLOSSARY

AIDS—acquired immune deficiency syndrome.

ANTIBODIES—proteins produced by the white blood cells of the immune system to fight pathogens.

ARBOVIRUSES—viruses that are transmitted by arthropods, such as ticks or mosquitoes.

ANTIRETROVIRAL (ARV)—any of a class of drugs used in the treatment of HIV/AIDS.

BACTERIUM (PLURAL: BACTERIA)—a round, spiral, or rod-shaped single-celled microorganism that lives in soil, water, organic matter, or plants and animals and that may cause disease.

ENDEMIC—prevalent or naturally present in a specific geographical region.

EPIDEMIC—a sudden occurrence of infectious disease affecting a large number of people over a short period of time.

GENERIC DRUG—a less expensive medication with the same properties as a brand-name drug (usually manufactured by a company that did not develop, and does not own the patent to, the brand-name drug).

HEMORRHAGIC—accompanied by hemorrhage, or massive bleeding from blood vessels.

HIV—human immunodeficiency virus, the virus that causes AIDS.

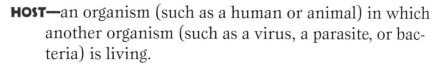
HOST—an organism (such as a human or animal) in which another organism (such as a virus, a parasite, or bacteria) is living.

LYMPHATIC SYSTEM—the network of nodes and vessels that maintain fluid levels and fight infections in the body.

MALNUTRITION—lack of nutrients (sugars, proteins, fats, vitamins, and minerals) needed for growth and good health.

OPPORTUNISTIC INFECTIONS—infections that cause disease only in people with weakened immune systems.

PANDEMIC—an epidemic that occurs over a wide geographic area and that affects a large proportion of the population.

PARASITE—an organism living in, with, or on another organism, especially when the host organism is damaged in the process.

PATHOGEN—a microorganism (such as a bacterium or virus) that causes disease.

POTABLE—suitable for drinking.

PROTOZOAN (PLURAL: PROTOZOA)—any of a type of single-celled organisms, some of which cause disease in humans and animals.

VECTOR—an organism, such as a fly, mosquito, or tick, that carries a pathogen from one host to another.

VIRUS—a microscopic disease-causing agent that is capable of reproducing only in the cells of living organisms.

FURTHER READING

Barnett, Tony, and Alan Whiteside. *AIDS in the Twenty-first Century: Disease and Globalization.* New York: Palgrave Macmillan, 2002.

Garrett, Laurie. *Betrayal of Trust: The Collapse of Global Public Health.* New York: Hyperion, 2000.

———. *The Coming Plague: Newly Emerging Diseases in a World Out of Balance.* New York: Farrar, Straus and Giroux, 1994.

Guest, Emma. *Children of AIDS: Africa's Orphan Crisis.* London and Sterling, Va.: Pluto Press, 2003.

Hoppe, Kirk Arden. *Lords of the Fly: Sleeping Sickness Control in British East Africa, 1900–1960.* Westport, Conn.: Praeger, 2003.

Hunter, Susan. *Black Death: AIDS in Africa.* New York: Palgrave Macmillan, 2003.

Naff, Clay Farris. *Vaccines.* Detroit: Greenhaven Press, 2005.

Preston, Robert. *The Hot Zone: A Terrifying True Story.* New York: Knopf, 1995.

Reichman, Lee B., and Janice Hopkins Tanne. *Timebomb: The Global Epidemic of Multi-drug-resistant Tuberculosis.* New York: McGraw-Hill, 2002.

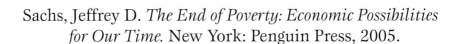

Sachs, Jeffrey D. *The End of Poverty: Economic Possibilities for Our Time.* New York: Penguin Press, 2005.

Stewart, Gail. *Tuberculosis.* San Diego: Lucent Books, 2002.

Willett, Edward. *Ebola Virus.* Berkeley Heights, N.J.: Enslow Publishers, 2003.

FURTHER READING

INTERNET RESOURCES

HTTP://WWW.AFRICARE.ORG

The website of this nonprofit organization provides information on the health status of many African nations.

HTTP://WWW.AFRO.WHO.INT

The Web page of the World Health Organization's regional office for Africa includes information on various diseases and health initiatives.

HTTP://WWW.CARTERCENTER.ORG

The "Health Programs" link on the website of the Atlanta-based humanitarian foundation provides information on river blindness, trachoma, lymphatic filariasis, and schistosomiasis.

HTTP://WWW.MSF.ORG

Médicins Sans Frontières (Doctors Without Borders) is a humanitarian medical and aid agency than works primarily in developing countries. The website provides information on the group's activities.

HTTP://WWW.POLIOERADICATION.ORG

Contains background information on polio, strategies for its eradication, and an up-to-date count of reported cases.

HTTP://WWW.THEGLOBALFUND.ORG

The website of the Global Fund to Fight AIDS, Tuberculosis and Malaria details the partnership's programs.

HTTP://WWW.UNAIDS.ORG

Background information on the UN agency and its efforts to address the AIDS pandemic.

HTTP://WWW.UNICEF.ORG/WHATWEDO/INDEX.HTML

This Web page from UNICEF includes information on immunization programs and the impact of HIV/AIDS on children.

HTTP://WWW.VACCINEALLIANCE.ORG

Website of the partnership of private- and public-sector groups working to save children's lives and protect public health through the worldwide use of vaccines.

INTERNET RESOURCES

FOR MORE INFORMATION

THE GLOBAL FUND TO FIGHT AIDS, TUBERCULOSIS AND MALARIA

Geneva Secretariat
53, Avenue Louis-Casaï
1216 Geneva-Cointrin, Switzerland
Tel: +4122 791 17 00
Fax: +4122 791 17 01
Website: www.theglobalfund.org

MÉDICINS SANS FRONTIÈRES (DOCTORS WITHOUT BORDERS)

333 7th Ave., 2nd Floor
New York, NY 10001-5004
(212) 679-6800
Fax: (212) 679-7016
Website: www.doctorswithoutborders.org

UNAIDS (JOINT UNITED NATIONS PROGRAM ON HIV/AIDS)

20, Rue Appia
1211 Geneva 27
Switzerland
Tel: +4122 791 35 11
Fax: +4122 791 41 79
Website: www.unaids.org

WORLD HEALTH ORGANIZATION (WHO)

Avenue Appia 20
1211 Geneva 27
Switzerland
Tel: + 41 22 791 10 82
Fax: + 4122 791 48 96
Website: www.who.it

FOR MORE INFORMATION

INDEX

Numbers in ***bold italic*** refer to captions.

PICTURE CREDITS

Front cover: Top Photos (left to right): Brent Stirton/Getty Images; Brent Stirton/Getty Images; Brent Stirton/Getty Images; Main Photo: Brent Stirton/Getty Images

Back cover: Back Cover: Collage of images created by OTTN Publishing with images provided by US AID

CONTRIBUTORS

PROFESSOR ROBERT I. ROTBERG is Director of the Program on Intrastate Conflict and Conflict Resolution at the Kennedy School, Harvard University, and President of the World Peace Foundation. He is the author of a number of books and articles on Africa, including *A Political History of Tropical Africa* and *Ending Autocracy, Enabling Democracy: The Tribulations of Southern Africa*.

LEEANNE GELLETLY is a freelance writer and editor living outside Philadelphia. She is a graduate of Muhlenberg College, in Allentown, Pennsylvania, and has attended classes at New York University, in New York, and at the Great Valley campus of Penn State University, in Malvern, Pennsylvania. Ms. Gelletly has worked in publishing for more than 20 years and has written on a variety of subjects. Her books include the biographies *Harriet Beecher Stowe* and *Mae Jemison*; geography titles that explore Bolivia, Colombia, and Somalia; and discussions of social issues such as Mexican immigration in the United States and violence in the media.